Vertigo

ALSO BY W.G. SEBALD
Available from New Directions

THE EMIGRANTS

THE RINGS OF SATURN

Vertigo

W. G. Sebald

Translated by MICHAEL HULSE

A NEW DIRECTIONS BOOK

Manufactured in the United States of America
New Directions Books are printed on acid-free paper.
First published clothbound in 2000
Published simultaneously in Canada by Penguin Books Canada Limited
Interior designed and typeset at Libanus Press, Malborough, Wiltshire, England.
Jacket design by Semadar Megged

Library of Congress Cataloging-in-Publication Data

Sebald, Winfried Georg, 1944-
[Schwindel, Gefühle. English]
Vertigo / W. G. Sebald ; translated by Michael Hulse.
p. cm.
"A New Directions book."
ISBN 0-8112-1430-3 (ak. paper)
I. Hulse, Michael, 1955-   II. Title.

PT2681.E18 S313 2000
833'.914—dc21
                                        99-058955

New Directions Books are published for James Laughlin
by New Directions Publishing Corporation
80 Eighth Avenue, New York 10011

CONTENTS

I

Beyle, or Love is a Madness Most Discreet

In mid-May of the year 1800 Napoleon and a force of 36,000 men crossed the Great St Bernard pass, an undertaking that had been regarded until that time as next to impossible. For almost a fortnight, an interminable column of men, animals and equipment proceeded from Martigny via Orsières through the Entremont valley and from there moved, in a seemingly never-ending serpentine, up to the pass two and a half thousand metres above sea level, the heavy barrels of the cannon having to be dragged by the soldiery, in hollowed-out tree trunks, now across snow and ice and now over bare outcrops and rocky escarpments.

Among those who took part in that legendary transalpine march, and who were not lost in nameless oblivion, was one Marie Henri Beyle. Seventeen years old at the time, he could now see before him the end of his profoundly detested

childhood and adolescence

and, with some enthusiasm, was embarking on a career in the armed services which was to take him the length and breadth of Europe. The notes in which the 53-year-old Beyle, writing during a sojourn at Civitavecchia, attempted to relive the tribulations of those days afford eloquent proof of the various difficulties entailed in the act of recollection. At times his view of the past consists of nothing but grey patches, then at others images appear of such extraordinary clarity he feels he can scarce credit them – such as that of General Marmont, whom he believes he saw at Martigny to the left of the track along which the column was moving, clad in the royal- and sky-blue robes of a Councillor of State, an image which he still beholds precisely thus, Beyle assures us, whenever he closes his eyes and pictures that scene, although he is well aware that at that time Marmont must have been wearing his general's uniform and not the blue robes of state.

Beyle, who claims at this period, owing to a wholly misdirected education which had aimed solely at developing his mental faculties, to have had the constitution of a fourteen-year-old girl, also writes that he was so affected by the large number of dead horses lying by the wayside, and the other detritus of war the army left in its wake as it moved in a long-drawn-out file up the mountains, that he now has no clear idea whatsoever of the things he found so horrifying then. It seemed to him that his impressions had been erased by the very violence of their impact. For that reason, the sketch below should be considered as a kind of aid by means of which Beyle sought to remember how things were when the part of the column in which he found himself came under fire near the village and fortress of Bard. *B* is the village of Bard. The three *C*s on the heights

to the right signify the fortress cannon, firing at the points marked with *L*s on the track that led across the steep slope, *P*. Where the *X* is, at the bottom of the valley and beyond all hope of rescue, lie horses that plunged off the track in a frenzy of fear. *H* stands for Henri and marks the narrator's own position. Yet, of course, when Beyle was in actual fact standing at that spot, he will not have been viewing the scene in this precise way, for in reality, as we know, everything is always quite different.

Beyle furthermore writes that even when the images supplied by memory are true to life one can place little confidence in them. Just as the magnificent spectacle of General Marmont at Martigny before the ascent remained fixed in his mind, so too, after the most arduous portion of the journey was done, the beauty of the descent from the heights of the pass, and of the St Bernard valley unfolding before him in the morning sun, made an indelible impression on him. He gazed and gazed upon it, and all the while his first words of Italian, taught him the day before by a priest with whom he was billeted – *quante miglia sono di qua a Ivrea* and *donna cattiva* – were going through his head. Beyle writes that for years he lived in the conviction that he could remember every detail of that ride, and part-icularly of the town of Ivrea, which he beheld for the first time from some three-quarters of a mile away, in light that was already fading. There it lay, to the right, where the valley gradually opens out into the plain, while on the left, in the far distance, the mountains arose, the Resegone di Lecco, which was later to mean so much to him, and at the furthest remove, the Monte Rosa.

It was a severe disappointment, Beyle writes, when some years ago, looking through old papers, he came across an engraving entitled *Prospetto d'Ivrea* and was obliged to concede that his recollected picture of the town in the evening sun was nothing but a copy of that very engraving. This being so, Beyle's advice is not to purchase engravings of fine views and prospects seen on one's travels, since before very long they will displace our memories completely, indeed one might say they destroy them. For instance, he could no longer recall the wonderful Sistine Madonna he had seen in Dresden, try as he might, because Müller's engraving after it had become superimposed in his mind; the wretched pastels by Mengs in the same gallery, on the other hand, of which he had never set eyes on a copy, remained before him as clear as when he first saw them.

At Ivrea, where the bivouacing army occupied every building and public square, he contrived to find quarters in the storehouse of a dyeing works for himself and Capitaine Burelvillers, in whose company he had ridden into the town. Their billet was amid all manner of barrels and copper vats, there was a curious acidic tang in the air, and Beyle had barely dismounted but he had to defend their quarters against a band of marauders bent on ripping off the shutters and doors for the camp fire they had lit in the yard. It was not only on account of this but indeed by virtue of all that had happened to him of late that Beyle felt he had come of age and, in a spirit of adventure, disregarding his hunger and weariness and the objections of the Capitaine, he set forth for the Emporeum, where that evening, as he knew from several public notices, *Il Matrimonio Segreto* was being performed.

Beyle's imagination, already in turmoil owing to the abnormal conditions then prevailing everywhere, was now further agitated by the music of Cimarosa. At the point in the first act where the secretly married Paolino and Caroline join their voices in the apprehensive duet *Cara, non dubitar: pietade troveremo, se il ciel barbaro non è*, he imagined himself not only on the boards of that rudimentary stage but indeed actually in the house of the deaf-eared merchant of Bologna, holding his youngest daughter in his arms. So profoundly was his heart stirred that, as the performance continued, tears came repeatedly to his eyes, and on leaving the Emporeum he was convinced that the actress who had played Caroline and who, he felt certain, had more than once bent her gaze most particularly on him, would be able to afford him the bliss promised by the music. He was not in the least troubled by the circumstance that when the soprano was grappling with the more difficult of the coloraturas, her left eye swivelled a little to the outerward, nor that her right upper canine was missing; quite the contrary, his exalted feelings seized upon these very defects. He knew now where happiness was to be sought: not in Paris, where he had supposed it dwelt when he was still in Grenoble, nor in the mountains of the Dauphiné, where on occasion he had longed to be when in Paris, but here in Italy, in this musical realm, in the beholding of such a divine actress. This conviction remained unshaken by the obscene jokes about the dubious morals of theatre ladies with which the Capitaine teased him the following morning as, leaving Ivrea behind, they rode on towards Milan and Beyle felt the emotion in his heart expanding to embrace the broad, rich landscape of early summer and the countless trees with their fresh green leafage that greeted him on all sides.

On the 23rd of September, 1800, some three months after his arrival in Milan, Henri Beyle, who until then had been performing clerical duties in the offices of the Embassy of the Republic in the Casa Bovara, was assigned to the 6th Dragoon Regiment with the rank of sub-lieutenant. Acquiring what was necessary in order to be correctly uniformed rapidly depleted his resources, since the cost of buck-leather breeches, of a helmet adorned from tip to nape with horsehair, of boots, spurs, belt buckles, breast straps, epaulettes, buttons and his insignia of rank far exceeded all his other expenses. This notwithstanding, it was with some satisfaction that Beyle now observed the figure he cut in his mirror, and, as he supposed, in the eyes of the Milanese women. He felt transformed, as if the high embroidered collar had lengthened his all too short neck and he had at last succeeded in shedding his unprepossessing body. Even his eyes, set somewhat far

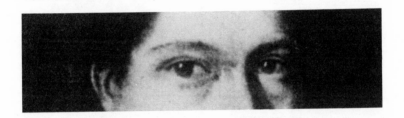

apart, on account of which, to his chagrin, he had often been called *Le Chinois*, suddenly seemed bolder, more focussed on some imaginary midpoint. And once fully apparelled in the uniform of a dragoon, this seventeen-and-a-half-year-old went around for days on end with an erection, before he finally dared disburden himself of the virginity he had brought with him from Paris. Afterwards, he could no longer recall the name or face of the *donna cattiva* who had assisted him in this task. The overpowering sensation, he wrote, blotted out the memory entirely. So thoroughly did Beyle serve his apprenticeship in the weeks that followed that in retrospect his entry into the world became a blur of the city's brothels, and before the year was out he was suffering the pains of venereal infection and was being treated with quicksilver and iodide of potassium; although this did not prevent him from working on a passion of a more abstract nature. The object of his craving was Angela

Pietragrua, the mistress of his fellow-soldier Louis Joinville. She, however, merely gave the ugly young dragoon the occasional pitying look.

It was not until eleven years later, when Beyle returned to Milan after a long absence and visited the unforgettable Angela once again, that he plucked up the courage to tell her of his exalted feelings. She scarcely remembered him. Somewhat discomfited by the passion of her unorthodox admirer, she attempted to ease the tension by proposing an excursion to the Villa Simonetta, where a widely famed echo would repeat a pistol shot up to fifty times. But this delaying tactic was of no avail. Lady Simonetta, as Beyle called Angela Pietragrua from that time on, at length felt compelled to capitulate before what seemed to her the insane loquacity Beyle displayed in her presence. All the same, she succeeded in exacting from him the promise that once he had enjoyed her favours he would depart Milan forthwith. Beyle accepted this condition without demur and left Milan, which he had missed for so long, that very same day, though not without recording, on his braces, the date and time of his conquest: 21 September at half past eleven in the morning. When the perennial traveller was once again seated in the diligence and the fine scenery was passing by, he wondered whether he would ever again carry off another such victory. As darkness

fell, the now familiar melancholy stole upon him, feelings
of guilt and inferiority very similar to those that had first
given him real and lasting anguish at the close of 1800. That
whole summer, the general euphoria that had followed
upon the Battle of Marengo had borne him up as if on
wings; utterly fascinated, he had read the continuing reports
in the intelligencers of the campaign in upper Italy; there
had been open-air performances, balls and illuminations,
and, when the day had come for him to don his uniform for
the first time, he had felt as if his life finally had its proper
place in a perfect system, or at least one that was aspiring to
perfection, and in which beauty and terror bore an exact
relation to each other. Late autumn, however, had brought
dejection with it. Garrison duties increasingly oppressed
him, Angela seemed to have little time for him, his disease

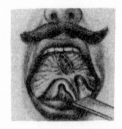

recurred, and over and over again, with the aid of a mirror, he
examined the inflammations and ulcers in his mouth and at
the back of his throat and the blotches on his inner thighs.

At the start of the new year, Beyle saw *Il Matrimonio Segreto* for the second time, at La Scala, but although the theatrical setting was perfect and the actress playing Caroline a great beauty, he was unable to imagine himself among the protagonists as he had in Ivrea. Indeed, he was now so far removed from it all that the music well-nigh broke his heart. The thunderous applause which shook the opera house at the close of the performance struck him as the final act in a process of destruction, like the crackling caused by a tremendous conflagration, and for a long time he remained in his seat, numbed by his hope that the fire might consume him. He was one of the last to quit the cloakroom, and in leaving he gave a parting glance at his reflection in the mirror and, thus confronting himself, posed for the first time the question that was to occupy him over the ensuing decades: what is it that undoes a writer? In view of the circumstances it seemed to him of particular significance when, a few days after that signal evening, he read in a gazette that on the eleventh of the month, in Venice, while working on his new opera, *Artemisia*, Cimarosa had suddenly died. On the 17th of January, *Artemisia* was given its première at the Teatro La Fenice. It was a huge success. Subsequently, strange rumours began circulating, to the effect that Cimarosa, who had been involved in the revolutionary movement in Naples, had been poisoned on the orders of Queen Caroline. Others speculated that Cimarosa had died as a result of the maltreatment he had suffered in the Neapolitan gaols. These rumours gave Beyle nightmares in which everything he had experienced in recent months was most horribly mixed up. They persisted undiminished, nor were they laid to rest when the Pope's personal physician, having especially conducted a post-mortem examination of Cimarosa's corpse, declared the cause of death to have been gangrene.

It was some considerable time before Beyle regained his peace of mind after these events. Throughout the early months of the year he suffered fevers and gastric cramps, which were treated partly with quinquina, partly with ipecacuanha and a paste of potash and antimony, whereupon his condition deteriorated to the extent that he more than once thought his end was nigh. When the summer arrived his fears, and with them the fever and the terrible stomach pains, gradually subsided. As soon as he was restored to a reasonable degree of health, Beyle, who had never been in any engagement except for his baptism of fire at Bard, set about visiting the places where the great battles of recent years had been fought. Time after time he traversed the landscape of Lombardy, of which he came to realise he had become exceedingly fond, with the grey and blue of distance

lying in ever more delicately nuanced bands until at the
horizon they dissolved into something resembling the haze
that hangs over the high mountains.

So it was that Beyle, on the way from Tortone, stopped
in the early morning of the 27th of September, 1801, on the
vast and silent terrain – only the larks could be heard as
they climbed the heavens – where on the 25th of Prairial
the previous year, exactly fifteen months and fifteen days
before, as he noted, the Battle of Marengo had been
fought. The decisive turn in the battle, brought about by
Kellermann's ferocious cavalry charge, which tore open the
flank of the main Austrian force at a time when the sun
was setting and all already seemed lost, was familiar to him
from many and various tellings, and he had himself pictured
it in numerous forms and hues. Now, however, he gazed
upon the plain, noted the few stark trees, and saw, scattered
over a vast area, the bones of perhaps 16,000 men and 4,000
horses that had lost their lives there, already bleached and
shining with dew. The difference between the images of
the battle which he had in his head and what he now saw
before him as evidence that the battle had in fact taken
place occasioned in him a vertiginous sense of confusion
such as he had never previously experienced. It may have
been for that reason that the memorial column that had

been erected on the battlefield made on him what he describes as an extremely mean impression. In its shabbiness, it fitted neither with his conception of the turbulence of the Battle of Marengo nor with the vast field of the dead on which he was now standing, alone with himself, like one meeting his doom.

Later, thinking back to that September day on the field of Marengo, it often seemed to Beyle as if he had foreseen the years which lay ahead, all the campaigns and disasters, even the fall and exile of Napoleon, and as if he had realised then that he would not find his fortune serving in the army. At all events, it was in the autumn that he resolved to become the greatest writer of all time. He did not, however, take any decisive steps towards the fulfilment of that ambition until Napoleon's empire began to crumble, nor did he make a first real advance into the world of literature until in the spring of 1820 he wrote *De l'Amour*, a kind of resumé of the hopeful yet disconcerting years that had gone before.

In March 1818, Beyle, who at that period often travelled to and fro between France and Italy, as indeed he did at other times in his life, met Métilde Dembowski Viscontini at her salon in Milan. Métilde, married to a Polish officer almost thirty years her senior, was twenty-eight and a woman of great, melancholy beauty. After about a year had passed, during which time he was one of the regular visitors at the houses on Piazza delle Galline and Piazza Belgioioso, Beyle's unspoken, discreet passion was on the point of winning the affection of Métilde, when he himself, as he later admitted, dashed his hopes by committing a blunder for which he could never make amends.

Métilde had gone to Volterra to visit her two sons, who were at the monastery school of San Michele there, and Beyle, unable to endure even a few days without seeing her, followed incognito. He was simply incapable of putting out of his mind his last glimpse of Métilde, on the eve of her departure from Milan. She had bent down in the hallway of her house to adjust her footwear, and, suddenly oblivious to everything else, he had beheld, in a profound darkness, as if through drifting smoke, a crimson desert behind her. This vision left him in a kind of trance, and it was in that state that he purchased the clothing he meant to wear as a disguise. He bought a new buff jacket, dark blue breeches, black patent leather boots, a velours hat with a more than usually high crown, and a pair of green spectacles, and in this attire he sauntered about Volterra, endeavouring to catch sight of Métilde at least from a distance as often as he possibly could. At first Beyle supposed himself unrecognised, only to realise, to his still greater satisfaction, that Métilde was giving him meaningful looks. He congratulated himself on this ingenious arrangement and from time to time, to a tune of his own devising, intoned the words *Je suis le compagnon secret et familier*, which struck him somehow as particularly amusing. Métilde, for her part, felt compromised by Beyle's conduct, as can readily be imagined, and, when his unaccountable behaviour finally became too vexatious, she sent him a dry note that put a fairly abrupt end to his hopes as a paramour.

Beyle was inconsolable. For months he reproached himself, and not until he determined to set down his great passion in a meditation on love did he recover his emotional equilibrium. On his writing desk, as a memento of Métilde, he kept a plaster cast of her left hand which he had contrived

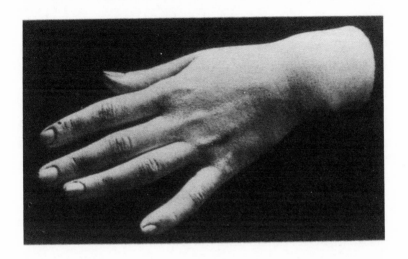

to obtain shortly before the débâcle – providentially, as he often reflected while writing. That hand now meant almost as much to him as Métilde herself could ever have done. In particular, the slight crookedness of the ring finger occasioned in him emotions of a vehemence he had not hitherto experienced.

In *De l'Amour* he describes a journey he claims to have made from Bologna in the company of one Mme Gherardi, whom he sometimes refers to simply as La Ghita. La Ghita, who reappears a number of times on the periphery of Beyle's later work, is a mysterious, not to say unearthly figure. There is reason to suspect that Beyle used her name as a cipher for various lovers such as Adèle Rebuffel, Angéline Bereyter and not least for Métilde Dembowski, and that Mme Gherardi, whose life would easily furnish a whole novel, as Beyle writes at one point, never really existed, despite all the documentary evidence, and was merely a phantom, albeit one to whom Beyle remained true for decades. It is further-more unclear at what time in his life Beyle made the journey with Mme Gherardi, always supposing that he made it at all. However, since there is much about Lake Garda in the opening pages of the narrative, it seems probable that some of what Beyle experienced in September 1813, when he was convalescing by the lakes of upper Italy, went into his account of the journey with Mme Gherardi.

In the autumn of 1813, Beyle was in a continuously elegiac frame of mind. The previous winter he had taken part in the terrible retreat from Russia, and afterwards had spent some time dealing with administrative business at Sagan in Silesia, where at the height of the summer he succumbed to a serious illness, during the course of which his senses were often confounded by images of the great fire of Moscow and of climbing the Schneekopf, which he had been planning to do immediately before the fever came upon him. Time after time Beyle found himself on a mountaintop, cut off from the rest of the world and surrounded by great squalls of snow driven horizontally through the tempestuous air and by the flames breaking from the roofs of burning houses.

The leave he took in upper Italy after recovering was marked by a sensation of debility and quietude, which caused him to view the natural world around him, and the longing for love which he continued to feel, in a wholly new way. A curious lightness such as he had never known took hold of him, and it is the recollection of that lightness which informs the account he wrote seven years later of a journey that may have been wholly imaginary, made with a companion who may likewise have been a mere figment of his own mind.

The narrative begins in Bologna, where the heat was so unbearable – in the early July of a year we cannot date precisely – that Beyle and Mme Gherardi decided to spend a few weeks breathing the fresher air of the mountains. Resting by day and travelling by night, they crossed the hilly country of Emilia-Romagna and the Mantuan marshes, shrouded in sulphurous vapours, and on the morning of the third day arrived in Desenzano on Lake Garda. Never in his entire life, writes Beyle, had the beauty and solitude of those waters made so profound an impression on him. Because of the oppressive heat, he and Mme Gherardi spent the evenings in a barque out on the lake, observing, during hours of unforgettable tranquillity, the most extraordinary gradations of colour as night fell. It was on one of those evenings, Beyle writes, that they talked of the pursuit of happiness. Mme Gherardi maintained that love, like most other blessings of civilisation, was a chimaera which we desire the more, the further removed we are from Nature. Insofar as we seek Nature solely in another body, we become cut off from Her; for love, she declared, is a passion that pays its debts in a coin of its own minting, and thus a purely notional transaction which one no more needs for one's fulfilment than one needs the instrument for trimming goose-quills that he, Beyle, had bought in Modena. Or do you imagine (thus, according to Beyle, she continued) that Petrarch was unhappy merely because he never knew the taste of coffee?

A few days after this conversation, Beyle and Mme Gherardi continued on their journey. Since the breezes traverse Lake Garda from north to south around midnight but from south to north in the hours before dawn, they first rode along the bank as far as Gargnano, halfway up the lake shore, and from there took a boat aboard which, as day broke, they entered the small port of Riva, where two boys were already sitting on the harbour wall playing dice.

Beyle drew Mme Gherardi's attention to an old boat, its mainmast fractured two-thirds of the way up, its buff-coloured sails hanging in folds. It appeared to have made fast only a short time ago, and two men in dark silver-buttoned tunics were at that moment carrying a bier ashore on which, under a large, frayed, flower-patterned silk cloth, lay what was evidently a human form. The scene affected Mme Gherardi so adversely that she insisted on quitting Riva without delay.

The further they penetrated into the mountains, the cooler and greener the landscape became, much to the delight of Mme Gherardi, for whom the dust-laden summers of her native city were so often an ordeal. That sombre moment in Riva, which crossed her memory like a shadow several times, was presently forgotten, and gave way to such high spirits that in Innsbruck, for the sheer pleasure of it, she bought a broad-brimmed Tyrolean hat of the kind familiar to us from pictures showing Andreas Hofer's rebellion, and persuaded Beyle, who had been meaning to turn back at this point, to continue further down the Inn valley with her, past Schwaz and Kufstein and onwards to Salzburg. There they stayed for several days, visiting the famed underground galleries of the Hallein salt mines, where one of the miners made Mme Gherardi a present of a twig which was encrusted with thousands of crystals. When they returned to the surface of the earth once again, Beyle writes, the rays of the sun set off in it a manifold glittering such as he had only seen flashing from diamonds as ladies revolved with their partners in a ballroom blazing with light.

The protracted crystallisation process, which had transformed the dead twig into a truly miraculous object, appeared to Beyle, by his own account, as an allegory for the growth of love in the salt mines of the soul. He expounded this idea at length to Mme Gherardi. She for her part, however, was not prepared to sacrifice the childish bliss that filled her that day in order to explore with Beyle the deeper meaning of what was doubtless a very pretty allegory, as she sardonically put it. Beyle took this as another example of the obstacles that so often appeared in his path as he continued his quest for a woman who might accord with his intellectual life, and he remarks that it was then he realised how even his most extravagant efforts would never be able to overcome those obstacles. In noting this, he broached a subject that was to occupy him as a writer for years to come. And so now, in 1826, approaching forty, he sat alone on a bench in the shade of two fine trees, enclosed by a low wall in the garden of the monastery of the Minori Osservanti high above Lake Albano and, with the cane he

now generally carried with him, slowly inscribed the initials of his former lovers in the dust, like the enigmatic runes of his life. The initials stand for Virginie Kubly, Angela

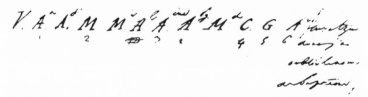

Pietragrua, Adèle Rebuffel, Mélanie Guilbert, Mina de Griesheim, Alexandrine Petit, Angéline (*qui je n'ai jamais aimé*) Bereyter, Métilde Dembowski, and for Clémentine, Giulia, and Mme Azur, whose first name he no longer remembered. Just as he no longer understood the names of these stars now unfamiliar to him, as he phrases it, so too it seemed ultimately incomprehensible to him, when he wrote *De l'Amour*, that whenever he tried to persuade Mme Gherardi to believe in love, she made him replies now of a melancholy sort, and now quite tart. It especially pained Beyle, however, at a time when he was beginning to accept with some reluctance the foundations of her philosophy, to find Mme Gherardi, as occurred often enough, according a certain value after all to the illusions of love he associated with the crystallisation of salt. At such moments he was horrified by a sudden awareness of his own insufficiency and a profound sense of failure. Beyle distinctly recalls that this horror came upon him on one occasion in the autumn of the year in which they had made their journey to the Alps together, when they were riding on the Cascata del Reno and discussing the torments the painter Oldofredi underwent in the name of love, which were then the talk of the town. Beyle had still not abandoned hope of winning the favour of Mme Gherardi, who was usually well disposed to his quick-witted conversation, and when she began to speak of a divine happiness beyond comparison with anything else in life, quite to herself as it seemed to him, a feeling of dread overcame him, and he described Oldofredi, doubtless thinking more of himself than of the painter, as a wretched foreigner. Thereupon he fell back, allowing the gap between his horse and that of Mme Gherardi – who, as has been remarked, may have existed only in his imagination – to widen steadily, and they rode the remaining three miles to Bologna without exchanging another word.

Beyle wrote his great novels between 1829 and 1842, plagued constantly by the symptoms of syphilis. Difficulties in swallowing, swellings in his armpits, and pains in his atrophying testicles troubled him especially. Having now become a meticulous observer, he kept a minute record of the fluctuating state of his health and in due course noted

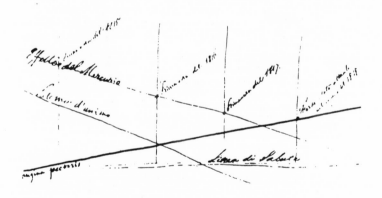

that his sleeplessness, his giddiness, the roaring in his ears, his palpitating pulse, and the shaking that was at times so bad that he could not use a knife and fork, were related not so much to the disease itself as to the extremely toxic substances with which he had dosed himself for years. His condition improved as little by little he stopped taking quicksilver and iodide of potassium; but he realised that his heart was gradually failing. As had long been his habit, Beyle calculated, with growing frequency, the age to which he might expect to live in cryptographic forms which, in their scrawled, ominous abstraction, seem like harbingers of death. Six years

of arduous work still remained to him when he jotted down this impenetrable note. On the evening of the 22nd of March, 1842, with the approach of spring already in the air, he fell to the pavement in rue Neuve-des-Capucines in an apoplectic fit. He was taken to his apartments in what is now rue Danielle-Casanova, and there, in the early hours of the following morning, without regaining consciousness, he died.

II

All'estero

In October 1980 I travelled from England, where I had then been living for nearly twenty-five years in a county which was almost always under grey skies, to Vienna, hoping that a change of place would help me get over a particularly difficult period in my life. In Vienna, however, I found that the days proved inordinately long, now they were not taken up by my customary routine of writing and gardening tasks, and I literally did not know where to turn. Early every morning I would set out and walk without aim or purpose through the streets of the inner city, through the Leopoldstadt and the Josefstadt. Later, when I looked at the map, I saw to my astonishment that none of my journeys had taken me beyond a precisely defined sickle- or crescent-shaped area, the outermost points of which were the Venediger Au by the Praterstern and the great hospital precincts of the Alsergrund. If the paths I had followed had been inked in, it would have seemed as though a man had kept trying out new tracks and connections over and over, only to be thwarted each time by the limitations of his reason, imagination or will-power, and obliged to turn back again. My traversing of the city, often continuing for hours, thus had very clear bounds, and yet at no point did my incomprehensible behaviour become apparent to me: that is to say, my continual walking and my reluctance to cross certain lines which were both invisible and, I presume, wholly arbitrary. All I know is that I found it impossible even to use public transport and, say, simply take the 41 tram out to Pötzleinsdorf or the 58 to Schönbrunn and take a stroll in the Pötzleinsdorf Park, the Dorotheerwald or the Fasangarten, as I had frequently done in the past. Turning in to a coffee house or bar, on the other hand, presented no particular problem. Indeed, whenever I was somewhat fortified and refreshed I regained a sense of normality for a while and, buoyed up by a touch of confidence, there were moments when I supposed that I could put an end to the muted condition I had been in for days, and make a telephone call. As it happened, however, the three or four people I might have cared to talk to were never there, and could not be induced to pick up the receiver no matter how long I let the phone ring. There is something peculiarly dispiriting about the emptiness that wells up when, in a strange city, one dials the same telephone numbers in vain. If no one answers, it is a disappointment of huge significance, quite as if these few random ciphers were a matter of life or death. So what else could I do, when I had put the coins that jingled out of the box back into my pocket, but wander aimlessly around until well into the night. Often, probably because I was so very tired, I believed I saw someone I knew walking ahead of me. Those who appeared in these halluci-nations, for that is what they were, were always people I had not thought of for years, or who had long since departed, such as Mathild Seelos or the one-armed village clerk Fürgut. On one occasion, in Gonzagagasse, I even thought I recog-nised the poet Dante, banished from his home town on pain of being burned at the stake. For some considerable time he walked a short distance ahead of me, with the familiar cowl on his head, distinctly taller than the people in the street, yet he passed by them unnoticed. When I walked faster in order to catch him up he went down Heinrichsgasse, but when I reached the corner he was nowhere to be seen. After one or two turns of this kind I began to sense in me a vague apprehension, which manifested itself as a feeling of vertigo.

The outlines on which I tried to focus dissolved, and my thoughts disintegrated before I could fully grasp them. Although at times, when obliged to lean against a wall or seek refuge in the doorway of a building, I feared that mental paralysis was beginning to take a hold of me, I could think of no way of resisting it but to walk until late into the night, till I was utterly worn out. In the ten days or so that I spent in Vienna I visited none of the sights and spoke not a word to a soul except for waiters and waitresses. The only creatures I talked to, if I remember correctly, were the jackdaws in the gardens by the city hall, and a white-headed blackbird that shared the jackdaws' interest in my grapes. Sitting for long periods on park benches and aimlessly wandering about the city, tending increasingly to avoid coffee houses and restaurants and take a snack at a stand wherever I happened to be, or simply eat something out of paper – all of this had already begun to change me without my being aware of it. The fact that I still lived in a hotel was at ever increasing variance with the woeful state I was now in. I began to carry all kinds of useless things around with me in a plastic bag I had brought with me from England, things I found it more impossible to part with as every day went by. Returning from my excursions at a late hour, I felt the eyes of the night porter at my back subjecting me to a long and questioning scrutiny as I stood in the hotel lobby waiting for the lift, hugging the bag to my chest. I no longer dared switch on the television in my room, and I cannot say whether I would ever have come out of this decline if one night as I slowly undressed, sitting on the edge of the bed, I had not been shocked by the sight of my shoes, which were literally falling apart. I felt queasy, and my eyes dimmed as they had once before on that day, when I reached the Ruprechtplatz after a long trail round the Leopoldstadt that had finally brought me through Ferdinandstrasse and over the Schwedenbrücke into the first district. The windows of the Jewish community centre, on the first floor of the building which also houses the synagogue and a kosher restaurant, were wide open, it being an unusually fine, indeed summery autumn day, and there were children within singing, unaccountably, "Jingle Bells" and "Silent Night" in English. The voices of singing children, and now in front of me my tattered and, as it seemed, ownerless shoes. Heaps of shoes and snow piled high – with these words in my head I lay down. When I awoke the next morning from a deep and dreamless sleep, which not even the surging roar of traffic on the Ring had been able to disturb, I felt as if I had crossed a wide stretch of water during the hours of my nocturnal absence. Before I opened my eyes I could see myself descending the gangway of a large ferry, and hardly had I stepped ashore but I resolved to take the evening train to Venice, and before that to spend the day with Ernst Herbeck in Klosterneuburg.

Ernst Herbeck has been afflicted with mental disorders ever since his twentieth year. He was first committed to an institution in 1940. At that time he was employed as an unskilled worker in a munitions factory. Suddenly he could hardly eat or sleep any more. He lay awake at night, counting aloud, his body was racked with cramps. Life in the family, and especially his father's incisive thinking, were corroding his nerves, as he put it. In the end he lost control of himself, knocked his plate away at mealtimes or tipped his soup under the bed. Occasionally his condition would improve for a while. In October 1944 he was even called up, only to be discharged in March 1945. One year after the war was over he was committed for the fourth and final time. He had been wandering the streets of Vienna at night, attracting attention by his behaviour, and had made incoherent and confused statements to the police. In the autumn of 1980, after thirty-four years in an institution, tormented for most of that time by the smallness of his own thoughts and perceiving everything as though through a veil drawn over his eyes, Ernst Herbeck was, so to speak, discharged from his illness and allowed to move into a pensioners' home in the town, among the inmates of which he was scarcely conspicuous. When I arrived at the home shortly before half past nine he was already standing waiting at the top of the steps that ran up to the entrance. I waved to him from the other side of the street, whereupon he raised his arm in welcome and, keeping it outstretched, came down the steps. He was wearing a glencheck suit with a hiking badge on the lapel. On his head he wore a narrow-brimmed hat, a kind of trilby, which he later took off when it grew too warm for him and carried beside him, just as my grandfather often used to do on summer walks. At my suggestion we took the train to

Altenberg, a few kilometres up the Danube. We were the only passengers in the carriage. Outside in the flood plain there were willows, poplars, alders and ash trees, allotment gardens and occasionally a little house raised on pillars against the water. Now and then we caught a glimpse of the river. Ernst let it all go by without venturing a word. The breeze that came in at the open window played about his forehead. His lids were half closed over his large eyes. When we arrived in Altenberg we walked back along the road a little in the direction we had come and then, turning off to the right, climbed the shady path to Burg Greifenstein, a medieval fortress that plays a significant part not only in my

own imagination but also, to this day, in that of the people of Greifenstein who live at the foot of the cliff. I had first visited the castle in the late 1960s, and from the terrace of the restaurant had looked down across the gleaming river and the waterlands, on which the shadows of evening were falling. Now, on that bright October day when Ernst and I, sitting beside each other, savoured that wonderful view,

a blue haze lay upon the sea of foliage that reaches right up to the walls of the castle. Currents of air were stirring the tops of the trees, and stray leaves were riding the breeze so high that little by little they vanished from sight. At times, Ernst was very far away. For minutes on end he left his fork sticking upright in his pastry. In the old days, he observed at one point, he had collected postage stamps, from Austria, Switzerland and the Argentine. Then he smoked another cigarette in silence, and when he stubbed it out he repeated, as if in amazement at his entire past life, that single word "Argentine", which possibly struck him as far too outlandish. That morning, I think, we were both within an inch of learning to fly, or at least I might have managed as much as is required for a decent crash. But we never catch the propitious moment. – I only know that the view from Burg Greifenstein is no longer the same. A dam has been built below the castle. The course of the river was straightened,

and the sad sight of it now will soon extinguish the memory of what it once was.

We made our way back on foot. For both of us the walk proved too long. Downcast we strode on in the autumn sunshine, side by side. The houses of Kritzendorf seemed to go on forever. Of the people who lived there not a sign was to be seen. They were all having lunch, clattering the cutlery and plates. A dog leapt at a green-painted iron gate, quite beside itself, as if it had taken leave of its senses. It was a large black Newfoundland, its natural gentleness broken by ill-treatment, long confinement or even the crystal clarity of the autumn day. In the villa behind the iron fence nothing stirred. Nobody came to the window, not even a curtain moved. Again and again the animal ran up and hurled itself at the gate, only occasionally pausing to eye us where we stood as if transfixed. As we walked on I could feel the chill of terror in my limbs. Ernst turned to look back once more at the black dog, which had now stopped barking and was standing motionless in the midday sun. Perhaps we should have let it out. It would probably have ambled along beside us, like a good beast, while its evil spirit might have stalked among the people of Kritzendorf in search of another host, and indeed might have entered them all simultaneously, so not one of them would have been able to lift a spoon or fork again.

We finally reached Klosterneuburg by way of Albrecht-strasse at the upper end of which there is a gruesome building banged together out of breezeblocks and prefab panels. The ground-floor windows are boarded up. Where the roof should be, only a rusty array of iron bars protrude into the sky. Looking at it was like witnessing a hideous

crime. Ernst put his best foot forward, averting his eyes from this fearful monument. A little further on, the children inside the primary school were singing, the most appealing sounds coming from those who could not quite manage to hit the right notes. Ernst stood still, turned to me as though we were both actors on a stage, and in a theatrical manner uttered a statement which appeared to me as if he had committed it to memory a long time ago: That is a very fine sound, borne upon the air, and uplifts one's heart. – Some two years previously I had stood once before outside that school. I had gone to Klosterneuburg with Clara to visit her grandmother, who had been taken into the old people's home in Martinsstrasse. On the way back we went down Albrechtstrasse and Clara gave in to the temptation to visit the school she had attended as a child. In one of the classrooms, the very one where she had been taught in the early 1950s, the selfsame schoolmistress was still teaching, almost thirty years later, her voice quite unchanged – still warning the children to keep at their work, as she had done then, and also not to chatter. Alone in the entrance hall, surrounded by closed doors that had seemed at one time like mighty portals, Clara was overcome by tears, as she later told me. At all events, when she came out she was in such a state of distress as I had never seen her in before. We returned to her grandmother's flat in Ottakring, and neither on the way there nor that entire evening did she regain her composure following this unexpected encounter with her past.

The St Martin's home is a large, rectangular building with massive stone walls dating from the seventeenth or eighteenth century. Clara's grandmother, Anna Goldsteiner, who was afflicted with that extreme kind of forgetfulness which soon renders even the simplest of everyday tasks impossible to perform, shared a dormitory on the fourth floor. Through the barred, deeply recessed windows there was a view down onto the tops of the trees on the steeply sloping ground to the rear of the house. It was like looking upon a heaving sea. The mainland, it seemed to me, had already sunk below the horizon. A foghorn droned. Further and further out the ship plied its passage upon the waters. From the engine room came the steady throb of the turbines. Out in the corridor, stray passengers went past, some of them on the arm of a nurse. It took an eternity, on these slow-motion walks, for them to cross from one side of the doorway to the other. How strange it is, to be standing leaning against the current of time. The parquet floor shifted beneath my feet. A low murmuring, rustling, dragging, praying and moaning filled the room. Clara was sitting beside her grandmother, stroking her hand. The semolina was doled out. The foghorn sounded again. A little way further out in the green and hilly water landscape, another steamer passed. On the bridge, his legs astride and the ribbons on his cap flying, stood a mariner, signalling in semaphore with two colourful flags. Clara held her grandmother close as they parted, and promised to come again soon. But barely three weeks later Anna Goldsteiner, who in the end, to her own amazement, could no longer even remember the names of the three husbands she had survived, died of a slight cold. At times it does not take much. For weeks after we learned of her death I could not put out of my mind the blue, half-empty pack of Bad Ischl salt under the sink in her council flat in Lorenz Mandl Gasse and which she would never now be able to use up.

Footsore from our walk, Ernst and I emerged from Albrechtstrasse onto the town square, which sloped slightly to one side. For a while we stood irresolute on the curb in the dazzling midday sun before trying, like two strangers, to cross the road amid the infernal traffic, almost being run down by a gravel truck. Once we were on the shady side of the street we dived into a bar. At first the dark that enveloped us as we entered was so impenetrable for eyes accustomed to the glare outside that we were obliged to sit down at the first table we came to. Only gradually and partially did our sight return and other people become apparent in the gloom, some of them bent low over their plates, others sitting curiously upright or leaning back, but all of them without exception on their own, a silent gathering, the shadow of the waitress threading among them, as if she were the bearer of secret messages between the several guests and the corpulent landlord. Ernst declined to eat anything, and instead took one of the cigarettes I offered him. A time or two he appreciatively turned the packet with its English wording in his hands. He inhaled the smoke deeply, with the air of a connoisseur. The cigarette, he had written in one of his poems,

> is a monopoly and must
> be smoked. So that it
> goes up in flames.

And, putting down his beer glass after taking a first draught, he observed that he had dreamed about English Boy Scouts last night. What I then told him about England, about the county in East Anglia where I live, the great wheatfields which in the autumn are transformed into a barren brown expanse stretching further than the eye can see, the rivers up which the incoming tide drives the sea water, and the times when the land is flooded and one can cross the fields in boats, as the Egyptians once did – all of this Ernst listened to with the patient lack of interest of a man who has long been familiar with every detail he is being told. I then asked if he would write something in my notebook, and this he did without the slightest hesitation with the ballpoint which he took from his jacket pocket, resting his left hand on the open page. His head to one side, his brow furrowed in concentration, his eyelids half-closed, he wrote:

England.

England ist bekanntlich eine Insel für sich. Wenn man nach England reisen will braucht man einen ganzen Tag.

30. Oktober 1980.   Ernst Herbeck

England. England, as is well known, is an island unto itself.
Travelling to England takes an entire day. 30 October 1980.
Ernst Herbeck. – We left. It was not far now to the St Agnes
home. When we parted, Ernst, standing on tiptoe and
bowing slightly, took his hat from his head and with it, as
he turned away, executed a sweeping motion which ended
with him putting the hat back on; a performance which
seemed to be, at the same time, both childishly easy and an
astonishing feat of artistry. This gesture, like the manner in
which he had greeted me that morning, put me in mind
of someone who had travelled with a circus for many years.

The train journey from Vienna to Venice has left scarcely
any trace in my memory. For what may have been an hour
I watched the lights of the southwestern metropolitan
sprawl pass by, till at length, lulled by the speed of the train,
which was like an analgesic after the never-ending tramping
through Vienna, I fell asleep. And it was in that sleep, with
everything outside long since plunged into darkness, that
I beheld a landscape that I have never forgotten. The
lower portion of the scene was almost immersed in the
approaching night. A woman was pushing a pram along a
field track towards a group of buildings, on one of which,
a dilapidated pub, the name Josef Jelinek was painted in large

letters over the gabled entrance. Mountains dark with forests rose above the rooftops, the jagged black summits silhouetted against the evening light. Higher than them all, though, was the tip of the Schneeberg, glowing, translucent, throwing out fire and sparks, towering into the dying brightness of a sky across which the strangest of greyish-pink cloud formations were moving, while visible between them were the winter planets and a crescent moon. In my dream I was in no doubt that the volcano was the Schneeberg, any more than I doubted that the countryside, above which I presently rose through a glittering shower of rain, was Argentina, an infinitely vast and deep green pastureland with clumps of trees and countless herds of horses. I awoke only as the train, which for so long had been threading the valleys at a steady pace, was racing out of the mountains and down to the plains below. I pulled down the window. Swathes of mist were ripping past me. We were hurtling onwards at breakneck speed. Pointed wedges of blue-black rock thrust up against the train. I leaned out and looked upwards, trying in vain to make out the tops of the fearful formations. Dark, narrow, ragged valleys opened up, mountain streams and waterfalls threw up white spray in a night on the edge of dawn, so close that their cold breath against my face made me shiver. It occurred to me that this was the Friaul, and with that thought came naturally the memory of the destruction which that region had suffered some few months before. Gradually the daybreak revealed landslides, great boulders, collapsed buildings, mounds of rubble and piles of stones, and here and there encampments of people living in tents. Scarcely a light was burning anywhere in the entire area. The low-lying cloud drifting in from the Alpine valleys and across that desolated country was conjoined in my mind's eye with a Tiepolo painting which I have often looked at for hours. It shows the plague-ravaged town of Este on the plain, seemingly unscathed. In the background are mountains, and a smoking summit. The light diffused through the picture seems to have been painted as if through a veil of ash. One could almost suppose it was this light that drove the people out of the town into the open fields, where, after reeling about for some time, they were finally laid low by the scourge they carried within them. In the centre foreground of the painting lies a mother dead of the plague, her child still alive in her arms. Kneeling to the left is St Thecla, interceding for the inhabitants of the town, her face upturned to where the heavenly hosts are traversing the aether. Holy Thecla, pray for us, that we may be safely delivered from all contagion and sudden death and most mercifully saved from perdition. Amen.

When the train had arrived in Venice, I first went to the

station barber's for a shave, and then stepped out into the forecourt of Ferrovia Santa Lucia. The dampness of the autumn morning still hung thick among the houses and over the Grand Canal. Heavily laden, the boats went by, sitting low in the water. With a surging rush they came from out of the mist, pushing ahead of them the aspic-green waves, and disappearing again in the white swathes of the air. The helmsmen stood erect and motionless at the stern. Their hands on the tiller, they gazed fixedly ahead. I walked from the Fondamenta across the broad square, up Rio Terrà Lista di Spagna and across the Canale di Cannaregio. As you enter into the heart of that city, you cannot tell what you will see next or indeed who will see you the very next moment. Scarcely has someone made an appearance than he has quit the stage again by another exit. These brief exhibitions are of an almost theatrical obscenity and at the same time have an air of conspiracy about them, into which one is drawn against one's will. If you walk behind someone in a deserted alleyway, you have only to quicken your step slightly to instil a little fear into the person you are following. And equally, you can feel like a quarry yourself. Confusion and ice-cold terror alternate. It was with a certain feeling of liberation, therefore, that I came upon the Grand Canal once again, near San Marcuola, after wandering about for the best part of an hour below the tall houses of the ghetto. Hurriedly, like the native Venetians on their way to work, I boarded a vaporetto. The mist had now dispersed. Not far from me, on one of the rear benches, there sat, and in fact very nearly lay, a man in a worn green loden coat whom I immediately recognised as King Ludwig II of Bavaria. He had grown somewhat older and rather gaunt, and curiously he was talking to a dwarfish lady in the strongly nasal English of the upper classes, but otherwise everything about him was right: the sickly pallor of the face, the wide-open childlike eyes, the wavy hair, the carious teeth. Il re Lodovico to the life. In all likelihood, I thought to myself, he had come by water to the *città inquinata Venezia merda*. After we had alighted I watched him walk away down the Riva degli Schiavoni in his billowing Tyrolean cloak, becoming smaller and smaller not only on account of the increasing distance but also because, as he went on talking incessantly, he bent down deeper and deeper to his diminutive companion. I did not follow them, but instead took my morning coffee in one of the bars on the Riva, reading the *Gazzettino*, making notes for a treatise on King Ludwig in Venice, and leafing through Grillparzer's *Italian Diary*, written in 1819. I had bought it in Vienna, because when I am travelling I often feel as Grillparzer did on his journeys. Nothing pleases me, any more than it did him; the sights

I find infinitely disappointing, one and all; and I sometimes think that I would have done far better to stay at home with my maps and timetables. Grillparzer paid even the Doge's Palace no more than a distinctly grudging respect. Despite its delicately crafted arcades and turrets, he wrote, the Doge's palace was inelegant and reminded him of a crocodile. What put this comparison into his head he did not know. The resolutions passed here by the Council of State must surely be mysterious, immutable and harsh, he observed, calling the palace an enigma in stone. The nature of that enigma was apparently dread, and for as long as he was in Venice Grillparzer could not shake off a sense of the uncanny. Trained in the law himself, he dwelt on that palace where the legal authorities resided and in the inmost cavern of which, as he put it, the Invisible Principle brooded. And those who had faded away, the persecutors and the persecuted, the murderers and the victims, rose up before him with their heads enshrouded. Shivers of fever beset the poor hypersensitive man.

One of the victims of Venetian justice was Giacomo Casanova. His *Histoire de ma fuite des prisons de la République de Venise qu'on appelle Les Plombs écrite à Dux en Bohème l'année 1787*, first published in Prague in 1788, affords an excellent insight into the inventiveness of penal justice at the time. For example, Casanova describes a type of garrotte. The victim is positioned with his back to a wall on which a horseshoe-shaped brace is mounted, and his head is jammed into this brace in such a way that it half encloses the neck. A silken band is passed around the neck and secured to a spool which a henchman turns slowly till at length the last throes of the condemned man are over. This strangulating apparatus is in the prison chambers below the lead roofs of the Doge's Palace. Casanova was in his thirtieth year when he was taken there. On the morning of the 26th of July, 1755, the Messergrande entered his room. Casanova was ordered to surrender any writings by himself or others that he possessed, to get dressed and to follow the Messergrande. The word "tribunal", he writes, completely paralysed me and left me only such physical strength as was essential if I were to obey. Mechanically he performed his ablutions and donned his best shirt and a new coat that had only just left the tailor's hands, as if he were off to a wedding. Shortly after he found himself in the loft space of the palace, in a cell measuring twelve feet by twelve. The ceiling was so low that he could not stand, and there was not a stick of furniture. A plank no more than a foot wide was fixed to the wall, to serve as both table and bed, and on it he laid his elegant silk mantle, the coat, inaugurated on so inauspicious an occasion, and his hat adorned with Spanish lace and an egret's plume. The heat was appalling. Through the bars, Casanova could see rats as big as hares scuttling about. He crossed to the window sill, from which he could see but a patch of sky. There he remained motionless for a full eight hours. Never in his life, he recorded, had the taste in his mouth been as bitter. Melancholy had him in its grip and would not let go. The dog days came. The sweat ran down him. For two weeks he did not move his bowels. When at last the stone-hard excrement was passed, he thought the pain would kill him. Casanova considered the limits of human reason. He established that, while it might be rare for a man to be driven insane, little was required to tip the balance. All that was needed was a slight shift, and nothing would be as it formerly was. In these deliberations, Casanova likened a lucid mind to a glass, which does not break of its own accord. Yet how easily it is shattered. One wrong move is all that it takes. This being so, he resolved to regain his composure and find a way of comprehending his situation. It was soon apparent that the condemned in that gaol were honourable persons to a man, but for reasons which were known only to their Excellencies, and were not disclosed to the detainees, they had had to be removed from society. When the tribunal seized a criminal, it was already convinced of his guilt. After all, the rules by which the tribunal proceeded were underwritten by senators elected from among the most capable and virtuous of men. Casanova realised that he would have to come to terms with the fact that the standards which now applied were those of the legal system of the Republic rather than of his own sense of justice. Fantasies of revenge of the kind he had entertained in the early days of his detention – such as rousing the people and, with himself at their head, slaughtering the government and the aristocracy – were out of the question. Soon he was prepared to forgive the injustice done to him, always providing he would some day be released. He found that, within certain limits, he was able to reach an accommodation with the powers who had confined him in that place. Everyday necessities, food and a few books were brought to his cell, at his own expense. In early November the great earthquake hit Lisbon, raising tidal waves as far away as Holland. One of the sturdiest roof joists visible through the window of Casanova's gaol began to turn, only to move back to its former position. After this, with no means of knowing whether his sentence might not be life, he abandoned all hope of release. All his thinking was now directed to preparing his escape from prison, and this occupied him for a full year. He was now permitted to take a daily walk around the attics, where a good deal of lumber lay about, and contrived to obtain a number of things that could serve his purpose. He came across piles of old ledgers with records of trials held in the previous century. They contained charges brought against confessors who had extorted penances for improper ends of their own, described in detail the habits of schoolmasters convicted of pederasty, and were full of the most extraordinary accounts of transgressions, evidently detailed for the delectation solely of the legal profession. Casanova observed that one kind of case that occurred with particular frequency in those old pages concerned the deflowering of virgins in the city's orphanages, among them the very one whose young ladies were heard every day in Santa Maria della Visitazione, on the Riva degli Schiavoni, uplifting their voices to the ceiling fresco of the three cardinal virtues, to which Tiepolo had put the finishing touches shortly after Casanova was arrested. No doubt the dispensation of justice in those days, as also in later times, was largely concerned with regulating the libidinous instinct, and presumably not a few of the prisoners slowly perishing beneath the leaden roof of the palace will have been of that irrepressible species whose desires drive them on, time after time, to the very same point.

In the autumn of his second year of imprisonment, Casanova's preparations had reached the stage at which he could contemplate an escape. The moment was propitious, since the inquisitors were to cross to the *terra firma* at that time, and Lorenzo, the warder, always got drunk when his superiors were away. In order to decide on the precise day and hour, Casanova consulted Ariosto's *Orlando Furioso*, using a system comparable to the *Sortes Virgilianae*. First he wrote down his question, then he derived numbers from the words and arranged these in an inverse pyramid, and finally, in a threefold procedure that involved subtracting nine from every pair of figures, he arrived at the first line of the seventh stanza of the ninth canto of *Orlando Furioso*, which runs: *Tra il fin d'ottobre e il capo di novembre.* This instruction, pinpointing the very hour, was the all-decisive sign Casanova had wanted, for he believed that a law was at work in so extraordinary a coincidence, inaccessible to even the most incisive thought, to which he must therefore defer. For my part, Casanova's attempt to plumb the unknown by means of a seemingly random operation of words and numbers later caused me to leaf back through my own diary for that year, whereupon I discovered to my amazement, and indeed to my considerable alarm, that the day in 1980 on which I was reading Grillparzer's journal in a bar on the Riva degli Schiavoni between the Danieli and Santa Maria della Visitazione, in other words near the Doge's Palace, was

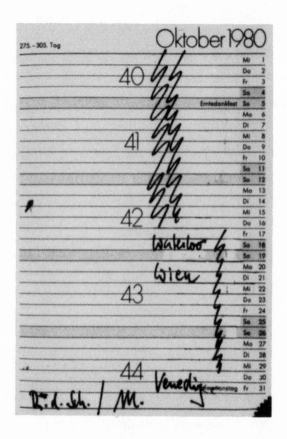

the very last day of October, and thus the anniversary of the day (or rather, night) on which Casanova, with the words *E quindi uscimmo a rimirar le stelle* on his lips, broke out of the lead-plated crocodile. Later that evening I returned to the bar on the Riva and fell into conversation with a Venetian by the name of Malachio, who had studied astrophysics at Cambridge and, as shortly transpired, saw everything from a great distance, not only the stars. Towards midnight we took his boat, which was moored outside, up the dragon's tail of the Grand Canal, past the Ferrovia and the Tronchetto, and out onto the open water, from where one has a view of the lights of the Mestre refineries stretching for miles along the coast. Malachio turned off the engine. The boat rose and fell with the waves, and it seemed to me that a long time passed. Before us lay the fading lustre of our world, at which we never tire of looking, as though it were a celestial city. The miracle of life born of carbon, I heard Malachio say, going up in flames. The engine started up once more, the bow of the boat lifted in the water, and we entered the Canale della Giudecca in a wide arc. Without a word, my guide pointed out the Inceneritore Comunale on the nameless island westward of the Giudecca. A deathly silent concrete shell beneath a white pall of smoke. I asked whether the burning went on throughout the night, and Malachio replied: *Sí, di continuo. Brucia continuamente.* The fires never go out. The Stucky flour mill entered our line of vision, built in the nineteenth century from millions of bricks, its blind windows staring across from the Giudecca to the Stazione Marittima. The structure is so enormous that the Doge's Palace would fit into it many times over, which leaves one wondering if it was really only grain that was milled in there. As we were passing by the façade, looming above us in the dark, the moon came out from behind the clouds and struck a gleam from the golden mosaic under the left gable, which shows the female figure of a reaper holding a sheaf of wheat, a most disconcerting image in this landscape of water and stone. Malachio told me that he had been giving a great deal of thought to the resurrection, and was pondering what the Book of Ezekiel could mean by saying that our bones and flesh would be carried into the domain of the prophet. He had no answers, but believed the questions were quite sufficient for him. The flour mill dissolved into the darkness, and ahead of us appeared the tower of San Giorgio and the dome of Santa Maria della Salute. Malachio steered the boat back to my hotel. There was nothing more to be said. The boat docked. We shook hands. I stepped ashore. The waves slapped against the stones, which were overgrown with shaggy moss. The boat turned about in the water. Malachio waved one more time and called out: *Ci vediamo a Gerusalemme.* And, a little further out, he repeated somewhat louder: Next year in Jerusalem! I crossed the forecourt of the hotel. There was not a soul about. Even the night porter had abandoned his post and was lying on a narrow bed in a kind of doorless den behind the reception desk, looking as if his body had been laid out. The test card was flickering softly on the television.

Machines alone have realised that sleep is no longer permitted, I thought as I ascended to my room, where tiredness
soon overcame me too.

Waking up in Venice is unlike waking up in any other
place. The day begins quietly. Only a stray shout here
and there may break the calm, or the sound of a shutter
being raised, or the wing-beat of the pigeons. How often,
I thought to myself, had I lain thus in a hotel room, in
Vienna or Frankfurt or Brussels, with my hands clasped
under my head, listening not to the stillness, as in Venice,
but to the roar of the traffic, with a mounting sense of
panic. That, then, I thought on such occasions, is the new
ocean. Ceaselessly, in great surges, the waves roll in over the
length and breadth of our cities, rising higher and higher,
breaking in a kind of frenzy when the roar reaches its peak
and then discharging across the stones and the asphalt
even as the next onrush is being released from where it was
held by the traffic lights. For some time now I have been
convinced that it is out of this din that the life is being
born which will come after us and will spell our gradual
destruction, just as we have been gradually destroying what
was there long before us. Thus it was that the silence which
hung over the city of Venice that All Saints' morning seemed
wholly unreal, as if it were about to be shattered, while I lay

submerged in the white air that drifted in at my half-open window. The village of W., where I spent the first nine years of my life, I now remember, was always shrouded in the densest fog on All Saints' Day and on All Souls'. And the villagers, without exception, wore their black clothes and went out to the graves which they had put in order the day before, removing the summer planting, pulling up the weeds, raking the gravel paths, and mixing soot in with the soil. Nothing in my childhood seemed to possess more meaning than those two days of remembrance devoted to the suffering of the sainted martyrs and poor unredeemed souls, days on which the dark shapes of the villagers moved about in the mist, strangely bent-over, as if they had been banished from their houses. What particularly affected me every year was eating the *Seelenwecken*, the special rolls that Mayrbeck baked on those commemorative days only, precisely one apiece, for every man, woman and child in the village. These *Seelenwecken* were made of white bread dough and were so tiny that they could easily be hidden in a small fist. There were four to a row on the baking tray. They were dusted with flour, and I remember one occasion when the flour-dust that remained on my fingers after I had eaten one of these *Seelenwecken* seemed like a revelation. That evening, I spent a long time digging in the flour barrel in my grandparents' bedroom with a wooden spoon, hoping to fathom the mystery which I supposed to be hidden there.

On that first day of November in 1980, preoccupied as I was with my notes and the ever widening and contracting circles of my thoughts, I became enveloped by a sense of utter emptiness and never once left my room. It seemed to me then that one could well end one's life simply through thinking and retreating into one's mind, for, although I had closed the windows and the room was warm, my limbs were growing progressively colder and stiffer with my lack of movement, so that when at length the waiter arrived with the red wine and sandwiches I had ordered, I felt as if I had already been interred or laid out for burial, silently grateful for the proffered libation, but no longer capable of consuming it. I imagined how it would be if I crossed the grey lagoon to the island of the departed, to Murano or further still to San Erasmo or to the Isola San Francesco del Deserto, among the marshes of St Catherine. With these thoughts, I drifted into a light sleep. The fog lifted and I beheld the green lagoon outspread in the May sunshine and the green islets like clumps of herbage surfacing from out of the placid expanse of water. I saw the hospital island of La Grazia with its circular panoptic building, from the windows of which thousands of madmen were waving, as though they were aboard a great ship sailing away. St Francis lay face down in the water of a trembling reed-bed, and across the swamps St Catherine came walking, in her hand a model of the wheel on which she had been broken. It was mounted on a stick and went round in the wind with a humming sound. The crimson dusk gathered above the lagoon, and when I awoke I lay in deep darkness. I thought about what Malachio had meant by *Ci vediamo a Gerusalemme*, tried in vain to recall his face or his eyes, and wondered whether I should go back to the bar on the Riva, but the more I deliberated, the less was I able to make any move at all. The second night in Venice went by, then All Souls' Day, and a third night, and not until the Monday morning did I come round, in a curious condition of weightlessness. A hot bath, yesterday's sandwiches and red wine, and a newspaper I had asked for, restored me sufficiently to be able to pack my bag and be on my way again.

The buffet at Santa Lucia station was surrounded by an infernal upheaval. A steadfast island, it held out against a crowd of people swaying like a field of corn in the wind, passing in and out of the doors, pushing against the food counter, and surging on to the cashiers who sat some way off at their elevated posts. If one did not have a ticket, one had to shout up to these enthroned women, who, clad only in the thinnest of overalls, with curled-up hair and half-lowered gaze, appeared to float, quite unaffected by the general commotion, above the heads of the supplicants and would pick out at random one of the pleas emerging from this crossfire of voices, repeat it over the uproar with a loud assurance that denied all possibility of doubt, and then, bending down a little, indulgent and at the same time disdainful, hand over the ticket together with the change. Once in possession of this scrap of paper, which had by now come to seem a matter of life and death, one had to fight one's way out of the crowd and across to the middle of the cafeteria, where the male employees of this awesome gastronomic establishment, positioned behind a circular food counter, faced the jostling masses with withering contempt, performing their duties in an unperturbed manner which, given the prevailing panic, gave an impression of a film in slow motion. In their freshly starched white linen jackets, this impassive corps of attendants, like their sisters, mothers and daughters at the cash registers, resembled some strange company of higher beings sitting in judgement, under the rules of an obscure system, on the endemic greed of a corrupted species, an impression that was reinforced by the fact that the buffet reached only to the waists of these earnest, white-aproned men, who were evidently standing on a raised platform inside the circle, whereas the clients on the outside could barely see over the counter. The staff, remarkably restrained as they appeared, had a way of setting down the glasses, saucers and ashtrays on the marble surface with such vehemence, it seemed they were determined to all but shatter them. My cappuccino was served, and for a moment I felt that having achieved this distinction constituted the supreme victory of my life. I surveyed the scene and immediately saw my mistake, for the people around me now looked like a circle of severed heads. I should not have been surprised, and indeed it would have seemed justified, even as I expired, if one of the white-breasted waiters had swept those severed heads, my own not excepted, off the smooth marble top into a knacker's pit, since every single one of them was intent on gorging itself to the last. A prey to unpleasant observations and far-fetched notions of this sort, I suddenly had a feeling that, amid this circle of spectres consuming their *colazione*, I had attracted somebody's attention. And indeed it transpired that the eyes of two young men were on me. They were leaning on the bar across from me, the one with his chin propped in his right hand, the other in his left. Just as the shadow of a cloud passes across a field, so the fear passed across my mind that these two men who were looking at me now had already crossed my path more than once since my arrival in Venice. They had also been in the bar on the Riva where I had met Malachio. The hands of the clock moved towards half past ten. I finished my cappuccino, went out to the platform, glancing back over my shoulder now and then, and boarded the train for Milan as I had intended.

I travelled as far as Verona, and there, having taken a room at the Golden Dove, went immediately to the Giardino Giusti, a long-standing habit of mine. There I spent the early

GIARDINO GIUSTI
VERONA
—

BIGLIETTO D'INGRESSO

№ 52314

hours of the afternoon lying on a stone bench below a cedar tree. I heard the soughing of the breeze among the branches and the delicate sound of the gardener raking the gravel paths between the low box hedges, the subtle scent of which still filled the air even in autumn. I had not experienced such a sense of well-being for a long time. Nonetheless, I got up after a while. As I left the gardens I paused to watch a pair of white Turkish doves soaring again and again into the sky above the treetops with only a few brisk wing-beats, remaining at those blue heights for a small eternity, and then, dropping with a barely audible gurgling call, gliding down on the air in sweeping arcs around the lovely cypresses, some of which had been growing there for as long as two hundred years. The everlasting green of the trees put me in mind of the yews in the churchyards of the county where I live. Yews grow more slowly even than cypresses. One inch of yew wood will often have upwards of a hundred annual growth rings, and there are said to be trees that have outlasted a full millennium and seem to have quite forgotten about dying. I went out into the forecourt, washed my face and hands at the fountain set in the ivy-covered garden wall, as I had done before going in, cast a last glance back at the

garden and, at the exit, waved a greeting to the keeper of the gate, who nodded to me from her gloomy cabin. Across the Ponte Nuovo and by way of the Via Nizza and the Via Stelle I walked down to the Piazza Bra. Entering the arena, I suddenly had a sense of being entangled in some dark web of intrigue. The arena was deserted but for a group of late-season excursionists to whom an aged cicerone was describing the unique qualities of this monumental theatre in a voice grown thin and cracked. I climbed to the topmost tiers and looked down at the group, which now appeared very small. The old man, who could not have been more than four feet, was wearing a jacket far too big for him, and, since he was hunchbacked and walked with a stoop, the front hem hung down to the ground. With a remarkable clarity, I heard him say, more clearly perhaps than those who stood around him, that in the arena one could discern, *grazie a un'acustica perfetta, l'assolo più impalpabile di un violino, la mezza voce più eterea di un soprano, il gemito più intimo di una Mimi morente sulla scena.* The excursionists were not greatly impressed by the enthusiasm for architecture and opera evinced by their misshapen guide, who continued to add this or that point to his account as he moved towards the exit, pausing every now and then as he turned to the group, which had also stopped, and raising his right forefinger like a tiny schoolmaster confronting a pack of children taller by a head than himself. By now the evening light came in very low over the arena, and for a while after the old man and his flock had left the stage I sat on alone, surrounded by the reddish shimmer of the marble. At least I thought I was alone, but as time went on I became aware of two figures in the deep shadow on the other side of the arena. They were without a doubt the same two young men who had kept their eyes on me that morning at the station in Venice. Like two watchmen they remained motionless at their posts until the sunlight had all but faded. Then they stood up, and I had the impression that they bowed to each other before descending from the tiers and vanishing in the darkness of the exit. At first I could not move from the spot, so ominous did these probably quite coincidental encounters appear to me. I could already see myself sitting in the arena all night, paralysed by fear and the cold. I had to muster all my rational powers before at length I was able to get up and make my way to the exit. When I was almost there I had a compulsive vision of an arrow whistling through the grey air, about to pierce my left shoulderblade and, with a distinctive, sickening sound, penetrate my heart.

Over the days that followed I was occupied more or less exclusively with my study of Pisanello, on whose account I had in fact decided to travel to Verona. It is many years now since the paintings of Pisanello instilled in me the desire to forfeit everything except my sense of vision. What appealed to me was not only the highly developed realism of his art, extraordinary for the time, but also the way in which he succeeded in creating the effect of the real, without suggesting a depth dimension, upon an essentially flat surface, in which every feature, the principals and the extras alike, the birds in the sky, the green forest and every single leaf of it, are all granted an equal and undiminished right to exist. It was this long-standing affection for Pisanello which took me once more to the Chiesa Sant'Anastasia to look at the fresco which he had painted over the entrance to the Pellegrini chapel in the year 1435. The Pellegrini chapel, in the left transept, is no longer what it once was. The archway has been closed up with boards of wood that have been painted brown in a careless manner; and there behind a door the verger has her retreat, or perhaps even the room in which she lives. At all events, it was into that room that the verger, a woebegone woman who had well-nigh faded away from long years of silence and solitude, disappeared without a word after she had unlocked the heavy iron-studded main door at a little past four o'clock and had led me, the sole visitor to the church, down the nave, wraithlike and somewhat unsteady on her feet. During the time I spent looking at the fresco she reappeared at regular intervals, as if she were making a perpetual circuit, venturing a little way off into the darkness, only to return again, as she completed her orbit, into her snug. Very little daylight enters the transept of Sant' Anastasia. Even on the brightest of afternoons, the profoundest gloom prevails. Pisanello's painting over the archway of the former chapel languishes deep in the shadows, but by dropping a thousand-lire coin into a metal box it can be illuminated for a certain period which can sometimes seem very long and sometimes extremely short. Then one sees St George setting off to fight the dragon, taking his leave of the *principessa*. All that remains in the left half of the painting is the somewhat faded monster and two as yet flightless young. Bones and skeletons of animals and humans sacrificed to placate the dragon lie strewn around. The vacancy into which the fragment dissolves still conveys something of the terror which, long ago, must have filled the people of the Palestinian city of Lydda, according to the legend. The right portion of the fresco, the other principal part, is almost completely preserved. A landscape of a more northerly character rises (the word is suggested by the nature of the depiction) into a blue sky. A ship with billowing sails, making headway on an inlet, is the only element in the composition hinting at remoteness and distance; everything else is very much of the

present and of this world, the undulating land, the ploughed
fields, the hedgerows and hills, the city with its roofs, towers
and battlements, and – a favourite motif at that time – the
gallows with the hanged men dangling from it, which para-
doxically imparts something lifelike to the scene. The bushes,
bosquets and foliage are painted meticulously, and the
animals, to which Pisanello always gave the closest attention,
are also rendered with great care: the stork flying inland, the
dogs, the ram, and the mounts of the seven horsemen, among
them a Kalmuck archer with a painfully intense expression on
his face. In the centre of the painting is the *principessa* in a
gown of feathers and St George, the silver of whose armour
has peeled off, though his reddish gold hair still glows about
him. It is astounding how Pisanello contrived to set the wide

open eyes of the knight, already wandering sideways to the hard and bloody battle ahead, against the self-contained expression of the woman indicated by little more than a slight

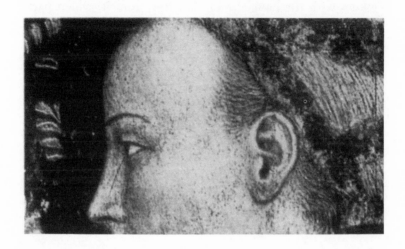

lowering of her gaze. On the third day of my stay in Verona, I took my evening meal in a pizzeria in the Via Roma. I do not know how I go about choosing the restaurants where I eat in unfamiliar cities. On the one hand I am too fastidious and wander the streets broad and narrow for hours on end before I make up my mind; on the other hand I generally finish up turning in simply anywhere, and then, in dreary surroundings and with a sense of discontent, select some dish that does not in the least appeal. That was how it was on that evening of the 5th of November. If I had heeded my first inclination, I would never have crossed the threshold of that establishment, which even from the outside made a disreputable impression. But now there I sat, on a kitchen chair with a cover of red marbled plastic, at a rickety table, in a grotto festooned with fishing nets. The decor of the floor and walls was a hideous marine blue which put an end to all hope I might have entertained of ever seeing dry land again. The sense of being wholly surrounded by water was rendered complete by a sea piece that hung right below the ceiling opposite me, in a frame painted a golden bronze. As is commonly the case with such sea pieces, it showed a ship, on the crest of a turquoise wave crowned with snow-white foam, about to plunge into the yawning depths that gaped beneath her bows. Plainly this was the moment immediately before a disaster. A mounting sense of unease took possession of me. I was obliged to push aside the plate, barely half of the pizza eaten, and grip the table edge, as a seasick man might grip a ship's rail. I sensed my brow running cold with fear, but was quite unable to call the waiter over and ask for the bill. Instead, in order to focus on reality once more, I pulled the newspaper I had bought that afternoon, the Venice *Gazzettino*, out of my jacket pocket and unfolded it on the table as best I could. The first article that caught my attention was an editorial report to the effect that yesterday, the 4th of November, a letter in strange runic writing had been received by the newspaper, in which a hitherto unknown group by the name of

ORGANIZZAZIONE LUDWIG

claimed responsibility for a number of murders that had been committed in Verona and other northern Italian cities since 1977. The article brought these as yet unsolved cases back to the memories of its readers. In late August 1977, a romany named Guerrino Spinelli had died in a Verona hospital of severe burns sustained when the old Alfa in which he customarily spent the night on the outskirts of the city was set on fire by persons unknown. A good year later, a waiter, Luciano Stefanato, was found dead in Padua with two 25-centimetre stab wounds in the neck, and another year after that a 22-year-old heroin addict, Claudio Costa, was found dead with thirty-nine knife wounds. It was now the late autumn of 1980. The waiter brought me the bill. It was folded and I opened it out. The letters and numbers blurred before my eyes. The 5th of November, 1980. Via Roma. Pizzeria Verona. Di Cadavero Carlo e Patierno Vittorio. Patierno and Cadavero. –

Pizzeria VERONA

Via Roma, 13 - Telefono 045122053   VERONA
Codice fiscale CRV CRL 58C13 F839R

di CADAVERO CARLO e RATIERNO VITTORIO
Abitazione: S. MARTINO B.A./ Verona - Via Piave, 61

Il *5 - 11 - 80*   № : 570

The telephone rang. The waiter wiped a glass dry and held it up to the light. Not until I felt I could stand the ringing no longer did he pick up the receiver. Then, jamming it between his shoulder and his chin, he paced to and fro behind the bar as far as the cable would let him. Only when he was speaking himself did he stop, and at these times he would lift his eyes to the ceiling. No, he said, Vittorio wasn't there. He was hunting. Yes, that was right, it was him, Carlo. Who else would it be? Who else would be in the restaurant? No, nobody. Not a soul all day. And now there was only one diner. *Un inglese*, he said, and looked across at me with what I took to be a touch of contempt. No wonder, he said, the days were getting shorter. The lean times were on the way. *L'inverno è alle porte. Sí, sí, l'inverno*, he shouted once more, looking over at me again. My heart missed a beat. I left 10,000 lire on the plate, folded up the paper, hurried out into the street and across the piazza, went into a brightly lit bar and had them call a taxi, returned to my hotel, packed my things in a rush, and fled by the night train to Innsbruck. Prepared for the very worst, I sat in my compartment unable to read and unable to close my eyes, listening to the rhythm of the wheels. At Rovereto an old Tyrolean woman carrying a shopping bag made of leather patches sewn together joined me, accompanied by her son, who might have been forty. I was immeasurably grateful to them when they came in and sat down. The son leaned his head back against the seat. Eyelids lowered, he smiled blissfully most of the time. At intervals, though, he would be seized by a spasm, and his mother would then make signs in the palm of his left hand, which lay in her lap, open, like an unwritten page. The train hauled onwards, uphill. Gradually I began to feel better. I went out into the corridor. We were in Bolzano. The Tyrolean woman and her son got out. Hand in hand the two of them headed towards the underpass. Even before they had vanished from sight, the train started off again. It was now beginning to feel distinctly colder. The train moved more slowly, there

were fewer lights, and the darkness was thicker. Franzensfeste
station passed. I saw scenes of a bygone war: the assault on the
pass – Vall'Inferno – the 26th of May, 1915. Bursts of gunfire
in the mountains and a forest shot to shreds. Rain hatched
the window-panes. The train changed track at points. The
pallid glow of arc-lamps suffused the compartment. We
stopped at the Brenner. No one got out and no one got in.
The frontier guards in their grey greatcoats paced to and fro
on the platform. We remained there for at least a quarter of
an hour. Across on the other side were the silver ribbons of
the rails. The rain turned to snow. And a heavy silence lay
upon the place, broken only by the bellowing of some nameless animals waiting in a siding to be transported onwards.

In the summer of 1987, seven years after I fled from Verona, I
finally yielded to a need I had felt for some time to repeat the
journey from Vienna via Venice to Verona, in order to probe
my somewhat imprecise recollections of those fraught and
hazardous days and perhaps record some of them. On this
occasion in the midst of the holiday season, the night train
from Vienna to Venice, on which in the late October of 1980
I had seen nobody except a pale-faced schoolmistress from
New Zealand, was so overcrowded that I had to stand in
the corridor all the way or crouch uncomfortably among

suitcases and rucksacks, so that instead of drifting into sleep I slid into my memories. Or rather, the memories (at least so it seemed to me) rose higher and higher in some space outside of myself, until, having reached a certain level, they overflowed from that space into me, like water over the top of a weir. Once I had begun to write, the time passed more swiftly than I should ever have thought possible, and it was not until the train was rolling slowly from Mestre over the railway causeway, crossing the lagoon which stretched out on either side in the gleam of the night, that I came to. At Santa Lucia I was one of the last to get out. With my blue canvas bag slung as ever across my shoulder, I slowly walked down the platform to the station hall, where a veritable army of backpackers were lying on the stone floor in sleeping-bags on straw mats, close to each other like an alien people resting on their way through the desert. Out in the station fore-court, too, countless young men and women lay in groups or couples or singly, on the steps and all around. I sat on the Riva and took out my writing materials, the pencil and the fine-ruled paper. The red glow of dawn was already breaking over the eastward roofs and domes of the city. Here and there, sleepers stirred in the no man's land where they had spent the night, propped themselves up and began to rummage through their belongings, eating a bite or drinking a little and then stowing it all carefully away again. Presently, bowed under heavy packs, which reached a full head above them, several began moving among their brothers and sisters still lying on the ground, as if they were preparing for the next stage of an arduous and never-ending journey.

I sat on the Fondamenta Santa Lucia until half the morning was gone. The pencil flew across the paper, and from time to time a cockerel crowed from its cage on the balcony of a house across the canal. When I looked up once again from my work, the shadowy forms of the sleepers on the station forecourt had all vanished, or had faded away, and the morning traffic had begun. At one point a barge laden with heaps of rubbish came by. A large rat scuttled along its gunnel and, having reached the bow, plunged head first into the water. I cannot say whether it was the sight of this that made me decide not to stay in Venice but to travel on to Padua instead, without delay, and seek out Enrico Scrovegni's Arena Chapel. Hitherto all I knew of it was an account that described the undiminished intensity of the colours in Giotto's frescoes, and the certainty which governs every stride and feature of the figures represented. Once I entered the chapel, from the heat that already prevailed in the city even in the early morning of that day, and stood before the three rows of frescoes that cover the walls up to the ceiling, I was

overwhelmed by the silent lament of the angels, who have
kept their station above our endless calamities for nigh on
seven centuries. Their lament resounded in the very silence
of the chapel and their eyebrows were drawn so far together
in their grief that one might have supposed them blindfolded.
And are not their white wings, I thought, with those few

bright green touches of Veronese earth, the most wondrous
of all the things we have ever conceived of? *Gli angeli visitano
la scena della disgrazia* – with these words on my lips I
returned through the roaring traffic to the station, not far
from the chapel, to take the very next train to Verona,
where I hoped to learn something not only relating to my
own abruptly broken-off stay in that city seven years before
but also about the disconcerting afternoon, as he himself
described it, that Dr K. spent there in September 1913 on
his way from Venice to Lake Garda. After barely an hour
of breezy travel, with the windows open upon the radiant

landscape, the Porta Nuova came into view and as I beheld the city lying in the semicircle of the distant mountains, I found myself incapable of alighting. Strangely transfixed, I remained seated, and when the train had left Verona and the guard came down the corridor once more I asked him for a supplementary ticket to Desenzano, where I knew that on Sunday the 21st of September,

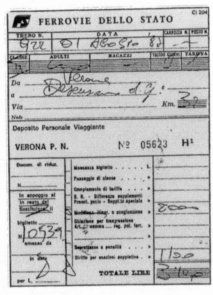

1913, Dr K., filled with the singular happiness of knowing that no one suspected where he was at that moment, but otherwise profoundly disconsolate, had lain alone in the grass on the lakeside and gazed out at the waves in the reeds.

The railway station at Desenzano, which cannot have been completed much before 1913 and which, at least externally, had changed little since, lay deserted in the midday sun when the departing train had shrunk to the size of the westerly vanishing point. Above the tracks, which ran towards the horizon in a straight line as far as the eye could see, the air shimmered. To the south were open fields. The station building, deserted though it seemed, gave a decidedly purposeful impression. Engraved in elegant lettering into the glass panels over the doors which faced the platform were the official designations of the station staff. *Capo stazione titulare. Capo di statione superiore. Capi stazione aggiunti. Manovratori manuali.* I waited in the hope that at least one representative of this bygone hierarchy, say, the stationmaster with a glinting monocle or a porter with a walrus moustache and long apron, would emerge from one of those doors and bid me welcome, but there was no sign of life. The building was deserted inside as well. For some time I wandered upstairs and down until I found the *pissoir*, where scarcely a thing had been altered since the turn of the century, as in the rest of the building. The wooden stalls in a military shade of green, the heavy stoneware basins and the white tiles had aged, were chipped and netted with hairline cracks, but otherwise everything was unchanged, except for the graffiti, all of which dated from the last twenty years. As I washed my hands I looked in the mirror and wondered whether Dr K., travelling from Verona, had also been at this station and found himself contemplating his face in this mirror. It would not have been surprising. And one of the graffiti beside the mirror seemed indeed to suggest as much. *Il cacciatore,* it read, in awkwardly formed letters. When I had dried my hands, I added the words *nella selva nera*.

Later on, I sat on a bench in the square outside the station for about half an hour, and had an espresso and a mineral water. It was good to sit in the shade, at peace in the middle of the day. But for a few taxi drivers dozing in their cabs and listening to their radios, there was no one in sight, until a *carabiniere* drove up, left his vehicle in the no parking zone immediately in front of the entrance, and disappeared into the station. When he emerged again, all the drivers got out of their taxis, as if at a signal, surrounded the somewhat undersized and slightly built policeman, whom they had perhaps known at school, and upbraided him on account of the illegal way he had parked. Barely had one said his piece but the next one began. The *carabiniere* could not get a word in, and whenever he tried he was promptly talked down. Helplessly, and even with a certain panic in his eyes, he stared at the accusing forefingers pointed at his chest. But since the entire performance merely served the taxi drivers as a timely diversion to dispel the midday boredom, their victim, for whom these accusations plainly went against the grain, could make no serious objection, not even when they set about faulting his posture and putting his uniform to rights, solicitously brushing the dust off his collar, straightening his tie and cap, and even adjusting his waistband. At length one of the drivers opened the police car door, and the guardian of the law, his dignity somewhat impaired, had no option but to climb in and drive off, tyres squealing, around the circle and down Via Cavour. The taxi drivers waved him off and stood around long after he was out of sight, reliving this or that part of the comedy, quite beside themselves with merriment.

Punctually, at a quarter past one, the blue bus I was to take to Riva arrived. I boarded it and took one of the seats in the middle. A few other passengers got on too, some of them locals, others travellers like myself. Not long before the bus departed at twenty-five past, a boy of about fifteen climbed aboard who bore the most uncanny resemblance imaginable to pictures of Franz Kafka as an adolescent schoolboy. And as if that were not enough, he had a twin brother who, so far as I could tell in my perplexed state of mind, did not differ from him in the slightest. The hairlines of both boys began well down their foreheads, they had the same dark eyes and thick brows, the same large and unequal ears, with the lobes growing into the skin of the neck. They were with their parents, and sat some way behind me. The bus started off, down Via Cavour. The branches of the trees lining the avenue scraped on the roof. My heart pounded, and a vertiginous feeling came over me as it used to in my childhood, when any car journey would make me feel sick. I leaned my head against the window frame, in the breeze, and for a long time did not dare look around. Not until we had left Salò far behind and were approaching Gargnano was I able to master the fright which had frozen my limbs and glance back over my shoulder. The two lads had not vanished, as I had partly feared and partly hoped they would have, but were half concealed behind an outspread newpaper, the *Siciliano*. A while later, summoning up all my courage, I tried to get into a conversation with them. Their only response to this was to grin witlessly at each other. Nor did I have any success, when I approached their parents, an exceptionally reserved couple who had already been watching my strange advances to their sons with mounting concern, in order to explain what the nature of my interest in these two sniggering boys actually was. The story I told them about a *scrittore ebreo* from the city of *Praga* who took the waters at Riva in the month of September 1913 and as a young man looked exactly – *esatto, esatto,* I hear myself repeating in despair, time after time – like their two sons, who were now and then peeping maliciously out from behind the *Siciliano*, evidently struck them, so their gestures conveyed, as pretty much the most incomprehensible nonsense they had ever heard. When at length, to dispel any suspicions they might have regarding my person, I said that I should be perfectly happy if they would send me, without revealing their name, a photograph of their sons to my English address once they had returned home from their holiday to Sicily, I realised that they were now quite certain that I must be an English pederast travelling Italy for his so-called pleasure. They informed me in no uncertain terms that they would not under any circumstances comply with my improper request and that they would appreciate it if I would return to my own seat right away. I realised that, if I did not, they would have been prepared to stop the bus in the next village and hand over this nuisance of a fellow passenger to the authorities. Grateful for every tunnel we had to pass through on the steep west bank of Lake Garda, I remained motionless on that bus seat from then on, embarrassed to the utmost degree and consumed with an impotent rage at the fact that I would now have no evidence whatsoever to document this most improbable coincidence. Continually I heard the sniggering of the two lads behind me, and in the end it was affecting me so badly that, when the bus stopped in Limone sul Garda, I took my bag down from the luggage net and got out.

It will have been close on four in the afternoon when,

weary and rather the worse for wear after the long journey from Vienna via Venice to Padua and then on to Limone, during which I had not slept at all, I entered the Hotel Sole on the lakeside, which at that time of day was deserted. One solitary visitor was sitting beneath a sunshade on the terrace, and inside, in the darkness behind the desk, stood the proprietress, Luciana Michelotti, also alone, jangling a small silver spoon absent-mindedly in an espresso cup that she had just drained. On that day, which as I later learned was her forty-fourth birthday, this woman whom I remember as resolute and zestful made a melancholy and even incon-solable impression. With a noticeable lack of urgency she dealt with my registration, leafing through my passport, perhaps intrigued at my being the same age as herself, repeatedly comparing my face with the photograph and at one point gazing long into my eyes, before finally locking the document carefully away in a drawer and handing me my room key. I was planning to stay for several days, do some writing, and rest a little. In the early hours of the evening, having found a suitable boat in the harbour with the help of Luciana's son Mauro, I rowed a good way out onto the lake. On the westerly side, everything was already sinking into the shadows that billowed down the steep cliff faces of the Dosso dei Róveri like dark curtains, and on the opposite east bank too the radiant evening light climbed the heights steadily, till all that could be seen was a pale pink glow over the peak of the Monte Altissimo. The whole of the darkly gleaming lake lay silently about me. The nocturnal noise of the loudspeakers on the hotel terraces and in the bars and discos of Limone, which had now begun, reached me as a mere dull pulsation, and seemed a negligible disturbance, measured against the huge bulk of the mountain that towered so high and steep above the quivering lights of the town that I thought it was inclining towards me and might tumble into the lake the very next moment. I lit the lamp in the stern of my boat and set myself rowing again, half towards the western shore and half against the cooling northerly breeze that passes over the lake every night. When I had reached the deep shadow of the rock wall, I shipped the oars, and drifted back slowly in the direction of the harbour. I extinguished the lamp, lay down in the boat and looked up into the vault of the heavens, where the stars were coming out over the glowering crags in such vast numbers that they appeared to touch one another. The rowing had left me aware of the blood coursing through my hands. The boat floated past the steep terraces of the derelict orchards where once upon a time lemons had been grown. In the darkness of these abandoned gardens, step by step scaling the heights stood hundreds of square stone pillars which once supported wooden cross-beams and the straw mats outstretched between them to protect the tender evergreen trees from the cold.

It was almost midnight in Limone when I got back into harbour again and walked round to my hotel. Holidaymakers were everywhere, in couples or family groups, a gaudy crowd moving like a cortège in procession through the narrow streets of the small resort locked between the lake and the sheer side of the mountain. Their sunburnt, painted faces swaying over the solid mass of their bodies were those of the wandering dead. Unhappy they seemed, every one of them, condemned to haunt these streets night after night. Back at my hotel I lay down on my bed and folded my arms under my head. There could be no prospect of sleep. From the terrace came the noise of the music and the confused blathering of the revellers, most of whom, as I realised with some dismay, were compatriots of mine. I heard Swabians, Franconians and Bavarians saying the most unsavoury things, and, if I found their broad, uninhibited dialects repellent, it was a veritable torment to have to listen to the loud-mouthed opinions and witticisms of a group of young men who clearly came from my home town. How I wished during those sleepless hours that I belonged to a different nation, or, better still, to none at all. Around two in the morning the music was turned off, but the last shouts and fragments of conversation did not die away until the first grey streaks of dawn were visible over the heights of the far shore. I took a couple of aspirin and fell asleep when the pain behind my forehead began to ease off, like the darkness that drains from the sand as the water recedes after high tide.

August the 2nd was a peaceful day. I sat at a table near the open terrace door, my papers and notes spread out around me, drawing connections between events that lay far apart but which seemed to me to be of the same order. I wrote with an ease that astonished me. Line by line I filled the pages of the ruled notepad I had brought with me from home. Luciana, at work behind the bar, threw me repeated sideways glances, as if to check that I had not lost my thread. She also brought me an espresso and a glass of water at regular intervals, as I had requested, and from time to time a toasted sandwich wrapped in a paper napkin. Often she would stand beside me for a while, making a little conversation, her eyes wandering over the written pages. On one occasion she asked if I was a journalist or writer. When I said that neither the one nor the other was quite right, she asked what it was that I was working on, to which I replied that I did not know for certain myself, but had a growing suspicion that it might turn into a crime story, set in upper Italy, in Venice, Verona and Riva. The plot revolved around a series of unsolved murders and the reappearance of a person who had long been missing. Luciana asked whether Limone featured in the story too, and I said that not only Limone but indeed the hotel and herself would be part of it. At this she beat a hasty retreat behind the bar, where she continued her work with that absent-minded precision that was peculiarly hers. Now she would prepare a cappuccino or hot chocolate, now pour a beer or glass of wine or grenadine for one of the few hotel guests sitting on the terrace during the daytime. Occasionally she would make entries in a large ledger, her head inclined to one side, looking for all the world as if she were still at school. More and more frequently I felt impelled to look over towards her, and whenever our eyes met she laughed as if at some silly inadvertence. On the wall behind the bar, between the colourful, shiny rows of spirits bottles, there was a large mirror, so I was able to watch both Luciana and her reflection, which gave me a curious satisfaction.

Around midday the guests disappeared from the terrace, and Luciana too left her post. The writing was becoming increasingly difficult, and soon it all seemed to be the most meaningless, empty, dishonest scrawl. I was greatly relieved when Mauro appeared, bringing the newspapers I had asked him to get me. Most of them were English and French, but there were also two Italian papers, the *Gazzettino* and the *Alto Adige*. By the time I was reading the last of them, the *Alto Adige*, the afternoon was almost over. A breeze was stirring the sunshades on the terrace, the guests were gradually returning, and Luciana had long since been busy behind the bar again. For a long while I puzzled over an article the heading of which, *Fedeli a Riva*, seemed to me to suggest some dark mystery, though the piece was merely about a couple by the name of Hilse, from Lünen near Dortmund, who had spent their vacations on Lake Garda every year since 1957. However, in the arts section of the paper I came across a report which did have a special meaning for me. It was a brief preview of a play that was due to be performed the next day

arabinieri «Casanova al castello di Dux»
di Selva   in scena domani al «Comunale»

in Bolzano. I had just finished reading this short article, underlining a thing or two, when Luciana brought me a Fernet. Once again she lingered, looking at the newspaper spread out before me. *Una fantesca*, I heard her say quietly, and I thought I felt her hand on my shoulder. It occurred to me then how few and far between in my life were the moments when I had been touched in this way by a woman with whom I was barely acquainted, and, thinking back, it seemed to me that about such unwonted gestures there had always been something disembodied and ghoulish, something that went quite through me! For example, I remember an occasion years ago, sitting in the darkened consulting room of a Manchester optometrist's and gazing through the lenses inserted into those strange eye-test frames at the letters in the illuminated box, which were in clear focus one moment, completely blurred the next. Beside me stood a Chinese optician whose name, so a small badge on her white overall told me, was Susi Ahoi. She said very little, but every time she leaned towards me to change the lenses I was aware of the cool aura of solicitude that surrounded her. Time and again she adjusted the heavy frame, and once she touched my temples, which as so often were throbbing with pain, with her fingertips, for rather longer than was necessary, I thought, though it was probably only in order to position my head better. Luciana's hand, which surely rested on my shoulder unintentionally, if it did so at all, as she leaned to take the espresso cup and the ashtray from the table, had a similar effect on me, and as on that distant occasion in Manchester I now suddenly saw everything out of focus, as if through lenses not made for my eyes.

On the following morning – I had decided to go over to Verona after all – it turned out that my passport, which Luciana had placed in a locker in the reception desk when I arrived, had gone astray. The girl who made up my bill, repeatedly stressing that she helped out at the hotel only in the mornings, rummaged in vain through all the drawers and compartments. At length she went to wake Mauro, who spent a quarter of an hour turning everything upside down and inside out and leafing through every one of the various passports kept at reception without finding mine, before fetching his mother down. Luciana gave me a long look when she appeared behind the desk, as if to say this was a fine way to take one's leave. Taking up the search for my lost passport, she said that the passports of all guests were kept in the same drawer, and not a single one had ever been mislaid since the hotel had been in existence. So the passport must be here in the drawer, and it was only a question of using one's eyes. But then, she told Mauro, he had never been any good at using his eyes, presumably because she, Luciana, had always used hers for him. Ever since he was small, if he couldn't find something right away – a schoolbook, his pencil case, his tennis racquet, his motorbike keys – he simply claimed it wasn't there, and whenever she, Luciana, had come to look, of course it *was* there. Mauro objected that she could say what she liked but this passport, at any rate, had vanished – *spa-ri-to*, he said, emphasising the individual syllables as if for someone hard of hearing. *Il passaporto scomparso* mocked Luciana. One remark led to another, and before long the argument started by my passport had escalated into a family drama. The *padrone*, too, whom till that moment I had not set eyes on and who was half a head shorter than Luciana, now arrived on the scene. Mauro told the entire story from the start, for the third time at least. The girl stood there without saying a word, continuously smoothing her pinafore with an embarrassed air. Luciana had turned away and, shaking her head and running her fingers through the curls in her hair, kept saying *strano, strano*, as if the disappearance of the passport, which could no longer be doubted, were the most extraordinary thing that had happened in all her life. The *padrone*, who had promptly embarked on a systematic search, placing all the Austrian, all the Dutch and all the German passports together, pushing the Austrian and Dutch

ones aside with a definitive gesture, and examining the
German ones closely, concluded from this operation that
while my passport was indeed not among them, there was,
in its stead so to speak, one which belonged to a certain Herr
Doll who, if he remembered correctly, had left yesterday and
must inadvertently have been given my passport – I still
hear him calling out *inavvertitamente*, striking his forehead
with the flat of his hand in despair at such negligence – and
that this Herr Doll had simply pocketed my passport without
checking whether it really was his own. Germans, declared
the *padrone*, concluding his account of these incredible
occurrences, were always in far too much of a hurry. Doubtless
Herr Doll was now somewhere on the motorway, and my
passport on his person. The question was now how I was to
be provided with provisional papers proving my identity, in
the absence of the passport, so that I could continue my
journey and leave Italy. Mauro, who appeared to be respon-
sible for the mix-up, apologised most profusely to me, while
Luciana, who now took his side, ventured that after all he
was still little more than a child. A child, exclaimed the
padrone, casting his eyes up to heaven as though requiring
support from that quarter in this hour in which his patience
was sorely tried – a child, he exclaimed again, but this time
to Mauro, a child he certainly is not, just mindless, and so,

without the least regard, he compromises the good reputation of our hotel. What will the *signore* think of Limone and Italy when he departs, the *padrone* demanded of Mauro, pointing to me, and, with the question still hanging in the air as quasi-irrefutable proof of my discomfiture, he added that I must now be taken without delay to the police station, where the police chief, Dalmazio Orgiu, would issue me with papers which would at least be valid for leaving the country. I put in that I could obtain a new passport at the German consulate in Milan and that there was no need to go to any further lengths on my account, but the *padrone* had already pressed the car keys into his wife's hand, picked up my bag and taken my arm. Before I knew what was happening I was sitting beside Luciana in the blue Alfa and we were driving up the steep streets to the main road, where the police station stood somewhat set back behind tall iron railings. The *brigadiere*, who wore an immense Rolex watch on his left wrist and a heavy gold bracelet on the right, listened to our tale, sat down at a huge, old-fashioned typewriter with a carriage practically a metre across, put in a sheet of paper and, half murmuring and half singing the text as he typed, dashed off the following document, which he tore out of the rollers with a flourish the moment he had completed it and read it over once more for good measure, handing it

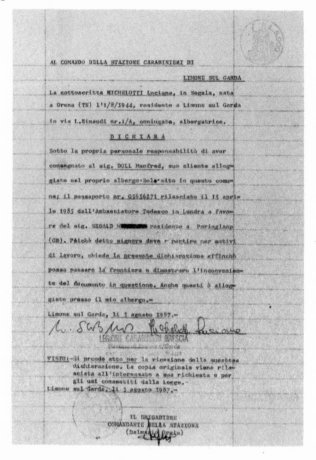

first to me, who was rendered speechless by this virtuoso performance, and then to Luciana for signature before endorsing it himself and, by way of completing the business, rubber-stamping it first with a circular and then with a rectangular stamp. When I asked the *brigadiere* if he were certain that the document he had drawn up would enable me to cross the border he replied, faintly irritated by the doubt implied in my question: *Non siamo in Russia, signore*.

When I was in the car with Luciana once again, the document in my hand, I felt as if we had just been married by the *brigadiere* and might now drive off together wherever we desired. But this notion, which filled me with intense pleasure, was short-lived, and once I had recovered my equilibrium I asked Luciana to drop me at the bus stop down the road. There I got out, and, my bag already slung over my shoulder, I exchanged a few more words with her through the open window of the car and belatedly wished her a happy forty-fourth birthday. She beamed as if at an unexpected present. Then, her head slightly inclined, she said *addio*, engaged the gears, and drove off. The Alfa glided slowly down the street and vanished around a bend which seemed to me to lead to another world. It was already midday. The next bus was not due till three o'clock. I went into a bar near the bus stop, ordered an espresso, and soon became so deeply absorbed in recasting my notes that I have not the faintest recollection either of the hours of waiting or of the bus journey to Desenzano. Not until I am on the train to Milan do I become visible again to my mind's eye. Outside, in the slanting sunlight of late afternoon, the poplars and fields of Lombardy went by. Opposite me sat a Franciscan nun of about thirty or thirty-five and a young girl with a colourful patchwork jacket over her shoulders. The girl had got on at Brescia, while the nun had already been on the train at Desenzano. The nun was reading her breviary, and the girl, no less immersed, was reading a photo story. Both were consummately beautiful, both very much present and yet altogether elsewhere. I admired the profound seriousness with which each of them turned the pages. Now the Franciscan nun would turn a page over, now the girl in the colourful jacket, then the girl again and then the Franciscan nun once more. Thus the time passed without my ever being able to exchange a glance with either the one or the other. I therefore tried to practise a like modesty, and took out *Der Beredte Italiener*, a handbook published in 1878 in Berne, for all who wish to make speedy and assured progress in colloquial Italian. In this little booklet, which had belonged to a maternal great-uncle of

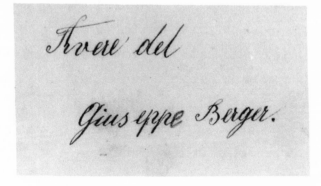

mine, who spent some time working as an office clerk in northern Italy towards the end of the last century, everything seemed arranged in the best of all possible ways, quite as though the world was made up purely of letters and words and as if, through this act of transformation, even the greatest of horrors were safely banished, as if to each dark side there were a redeeming counterpart, to every evil its good, to every pain its pleasure, and to every lie a measure of truth. Soon

the outlying districts of Milan came into view. Satellite developments with twenty-storey residential blocks. Then the suburbs, factory yards and older tenement buildings. The train changed to another track. The low rays of the setting sun passed through the compartment. The girl in the colourful jacket inserted a bookmark into her photo story, and the Franciscan sister also slipped a green ribbon into her breviary. Both now sat leaning back in the fullness of the evening glow, until at length we entered the darkness of the Central Station, and were all changed into amorphous shadows. As the train ground to a halt, the screeching of the brakes reached an excruciating pitch before it finally cut out and gave way to a moment of complete silence into which, almost at once, the heaving noise that prevailed under the great iron vaults flowed back. Filled by a sense of having been abandoned, I remained standing for a while on the platform. The girl in the many-coloured jacket and the Franciscan nun had long since disappeared. What connection could there be, I then wondered and now wonder again, between those two beautiful female readers and this immense railway terminus which, when it was built in 1932, outdid all other train stations in Europe; and what relation was there between the so-called monuments of the past and the vague longing, propagated through our bodies, to people the dust-blown expanses and tidal plains of the future. My bag slung over my shoulder, I strolled down the platform, the last of the passengers, and at a kiosk bought myself a map of the city. How many city maps have I not bought in my time? I always try to find reliable bearings at least in the space that surrounds me. The map of Milan I had purchased seemed a curiously apt choice, because while I was waiting for the quietly rumbling photo-booth where I had had some pictures taken to yield up the prints, I noticed on the front of the map's cardboard cover the black and white image of a labyrinth, and on the back an

affirmation that must seem promising and indeed auspicious for anyone who knows what it is to err on one's way:

UNA GUIDA SICURA PER

L'ORGANIZZAZIONE DEL VOSTRO LAVORO.

PIANTA GENERALE
MILANO

I emerged from the station hall into the leaden evening air. Yellow taxis came drifting towards their rank from every quarter, only to set off once again with more weary home-comers in the back. I walked through the colonnades to the eastern side, the wrong side of the station. Under the archway that gives onto the Piazza Savoia was a Hertz advertisement bearing the words LA PROSSIMA COINCIDENZA. I was still gazing up at this message, thinking it might possibly be meant for me, when two young men, talking to each other in a state of great agitation, came straight at me. It was quite impossible to get out of their way: their breath was already upon my face, already I was seeing the knotty scar on the one's cheek and the veins in the other's eye and feeling their hands beneath my jacket, grabbing, tugging and pulling. Not until I turned on my heel and swung the bag off my shoulder into the pair of them did I manage to disengage myself and retreat to one of the pillars in the archway. LA PROSSIMA COINCIDENZA. None of the passers-by had taken any notice of the incident. I, however, watched my two assailants, jerking curiously as if they were out of an early motion picture, vanish in the half-light under the colonnades. In the taxi, I clutched my bag with both hands. To my remark that Milan was dangerous territory, ventured in as casual a tone as I could muster, the driver responded with a gesture of helplessness. His nearside window was protected by a metal grille, and he had a multi-coloured medallion of Our Lady on the dashboard. We drove along the Via N. Torriani, across the Piazza Cincinnato, turned left into the Via San Gregorio and left again into the Via Lodovico, and drew up outside the Hotel Boston, which looked an unprepossessing, ill-omened house. The driver took the fare without a word and the taxi vanished in the distance. Nowhere in all the Via Lodovico was there a living soul to be seen. I climbed the few steps to the unappealing hostelry and waited in the dimly lit hallway until the *signora*, a wizen-faced creature of some sixty or seventy years, appeared from the television room. Suspiciously she kept her beady eye on me while I explained, in my halting Italian, that I was unable to show any papers because my passport had gone astray and I was in Milan to obtain a new one from the German consulate. As soon as I had finished my sorry tale she called her husband, who answered to the name of Orlando and who now also emerged unsteadily from the television room, where he had languished, like the *signora*, in something of a stupor. He took what seemed an age to cross the small lobby and take up his position beside his wife behind the reception desk, which came up nearly to their shoulders. When I told my story all over again, it no longer sounded plausible, even to me. Half in pity and half in contempt I was at length handed an old iron key bearing the number 513. The room was right at the top, but the lift, a cramped and clattering metal cage, went only as far as the fourth floor, from where I had to climb up two back stairs. A long corridor, far too long for that narrow building, led past a row of doors barely more than two metres apart down a slight incline, as it seemed to me. Poor travellers, I thought, seeing myself among them: always somewhere else. The key turned in the lock. An oppressive heat that had been building up for days and perhaps even weeks hit me. I pulled up the blinds. There were rooftops as far as the eye could see in the gathering dusk, and a forest of aerials stirred faintly in a breeze. Below, a chasm of backyards yawned. I turned away from this view and without undressing lay down on the bed, which was covered with a fringed, floral-patterned, damask spread, folded my arms under my head, and stared up at the ceiling, which appeared to be miles away. Stray voices drifted up from below and came in at the open window. A cry, as from someone swept out to sea, a shrieking laugh in an empty theatre. Time passed and it grew gradually darker. Little by little, the sounds subsided and there was silence. Hours went by, never-ending hours, but rest eluded me. In the middle of the night, or it may even have been towards morning, I got up, undressed and climbed into the shower cabin, which jutted into the room and was concealed behind a mildewed plastic curtain. For a long while I let the water run down me. And then, wet as I was, I lay down again on the fringed bedspread and waited for dawn to touch the tips of the aerials. At last I thought I could make out the first glimmer, I heard the call of a blackbird and shut my eyes. A pulsating glow spread under my lowered lids. *Ecco l'arcobaleno.* Behold the rainbow in the heavens. *Ecco l'arco celeste.* Sleep came and I dreamed of a green field of corn and floating above it, with outstretched arms, a convent nun from my childhood, Sister Mauritia, quite as if it were the most natural thing in the world.

At nine next morning I was in the waiting room of the German consulate in the Via Solferino. At that early hour there were already a considerable number of travellers who had been robbed and people with other concerns, among them a family of artistes who seemed to me to belong to an era that ended at least half a century ago. The head of this small troupe – for that was undoubtedly what they were – was wearing a white summer suit and extremely elegant canvas shoes with a brown leather trim. In his hands he was twirling a broad-brimmed straw hat of exquisite form, now clockwise, now anticlockwise. From the precision of his movements one knew that preparing an omelette on the high-wire, that sensational trick performed by the legendary Blondel, would have been mere child's play for this grounded tightrope-walker whose true home, one felt, was the freedom of the air. Next to him sat a remarkably Nordic-looking young woman in a tailor-made suit, she too straight out of the 1930s. She sat quite still and bolt upright,

All'estero

her eyes shut the whole time. Not once did I see her glance
up or notice the slightest twitch at the corners of her mouth.
She held her head always in the same position and not a
hair was out of place in her painstakingly crimped coiffure.
With these two somnambulists, whose names proved to be
Giorgio and Rosa Santini, there were three girls, all of about
the same age, wearing summer frocks of the finest cambric,
who resembled each other very closely. Now they would sit
quietly, now wander about among the chairs and tables in
the waiting room almost as if they were trying to make their
meanderings into intricate, beautiful loops. One of them
had a brightly coloured whirligig, one a collapsible telescope
which she tended to hold to her eye the wrong way round,
and the third a parasol. At times all three, with their sundry
emblems, would sit at the window and gaze out at the
Milanese morning, where the shimmering daylight was
breaking through the heavy grey air. Sitting apart from the
Santinis, though plainly with them, in her affections and by
relation, was the *nonna* in a black silk dress. She was busy
with crocheting and looked up only occasionally to cast what
seemed to me a worried look at the silent couple or the three
sisters. Although it took a long while until my identity
had been established, by several phone calls to the relevant
authorities in Germany and London, the time passed lightly

in the company of these people. At length, a short, not to say dwarfish consular official settled himself on a sort of barstool behind an enormous typing machine in order to enter in dotted letters the details I had given concerning my person into a new passport. Emerging from the consulate building

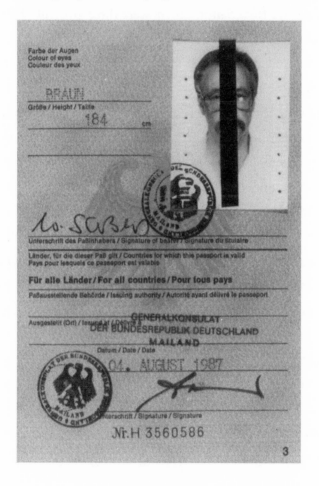

with this newly issued proof of my freedom to come and go as I pleased in my pocket, I decided to take a stroll around the streets of Milan for an hour or so before travelling on, although of course I might have known that any idea of the kind, in a city so filled with the most appalling traffic, will end in aimless wandering and bouts of distress. On that day, the 4th of August, 1987, I walked down the Via Moscova, past San Angelo, through the Giardini Pubblici, along the Via Palestro, the Via Marina, the Via Senato, the Via della Spiga, the Via Gesù, into the Via Monte Napoleone and the Via Alessandro Manzoni, by way of which I finally reached the Piazza della Scala, from where I crossed to the cathedral square. Inside the cathedral I sat down for a while, untied my shoe-laces, and, as I still remember with undiminished clarity, all of a sudden no longer had any knowledge of where I was. Despite a great effort to account for the last few days and how I had come to be in this place, I was unable even to determine whether I was in the land of the living or already in another place. Nor did this lapse of memory improve in the slightest after I climbed to the topmost gallery of the cathedral and from there, beset by recurring fits of vertigo, gazed out upon the dusky, hazy panorama of a city now altogether alien to me. Where the word "Milan" ought to have appeared in my mind there was nothing but a painful, inane reflex. A menacing reflection of the darkness spreading within me loomed up in the west where an immense bank of cloud covered half the sky and cast its shadow on the seemingly endless sea of houses. A stiff wind came up, and I had to brace myself so that I could look down to where the people were crossing the piazza, their bodies inclined forwards at an odd angle, as though they were hastening towards their doom – a spectacle which brought back to me an epitaph I had seen years before on a tombstone in the Piedmont. And as I remembered the words *Se il vento s'alza, Correte, Corrrete! Se il vento s'alza, non v'arrestate!,* so I knew, in that instant, that the figures hurrying over the cobbles below were none other than the men and women of Milan.

That evening I was on my way to Verona once again. The train raced through the dark countryside at an alarming speed. This time I alighted at my destination without a second thought and, once I had had a double Fernet in the station bar and browsed through the Verona newspapers, I took a taxi to the Golden Dove, where, contrary to all expectation, at the height of the season, a room perfectly suited to my needs was made available and where I was treated with exquisite courtesy, both by the porter, who reminded me of Ferdinand Bruckner, and by the hotel manageress, who seemed to be waiting in the foyer for the express purpose of welcoming me as a long expected guest of honour who had finally arrived. Rather than asking for my passport, she simply handed me the register, and I entered my name as Jakob Philipp Fallmerayer, historian, of Landeck, Tyrol. The porter picked up my bag and preceded me to the room, where I gave him a tip that far exceeded my means, at which he left with a deep bow. That night under the roof of the Golden Dove, I felt safe as if under the wing of a bird whose plumage I saw in the finest shades of brown and brick-red, a well-nigh miraculous reprieve, as was the breakfast next morning, which I recall as a very dignified occasion. Confidently, as if from now on I could not put a foot wrong, I set off shortly before ten through the city streets, and soon found myself outside the Biblioteca Civica, where I proposed to spend the day working. A notice on the main entrance advised the public that the library was closed during the holiday period, but the door stood ajar. Inside, it was so gloomy that at first I had to feel my way forwards. In vain I tried a number of door handles, all of which seemed curiously high to me, before at last I found one of the librarians in a reading room flooded with the mild light of the early morning. He was an old gentleman with carefully trimmed hair and beard, who had just settled down to the day's task behind his desk. He wore black satin armlets and gold-rimmed half-moon spectacles, and was ruling lines on one sheet of paper after another. Once he had prepared a batch, he looked up from the business in hand and enquired what it was I had come for. Having listened to my protracted explanation, he went to fetch what I wanted and before long I was sitting near one of the windows leafing through the folio volumes in which the Verona newspapers dating from August and September 1913 were bound. The edges were by now so brittle that the pages needed to be turned with much care. All manner of silent movie scenes began to be enacted before my eyes. In Via Alberto Mario I beheld divers gentlemen walking up and down and, at the very moment they supposed themselves unobserved, deftly side-stepping, with lightning alacrity, into the doorway of the building that housed the establishment of Dr Ringger, graduate of the medical schools of Paris and Vienna. Each of the many chambers within was already occupied by an impeccably suited gentleman of the sort that continued to leap in from the street, while Dr Ringger, for his part, was to be seen in the great salon on the mezzanine floor perusing, in preparation for his surgery hours, a range of outsize pictorial reproductions of the inflorescences caused by diseases of the skin, spread out before him on a huge table like the multi-coloured ordnance maps at a war council of the general staff. And then I witnessed Dr Pesavento, whose practice was in the Via Stella, not far from the Biblioteca Civica, performing one of his painless

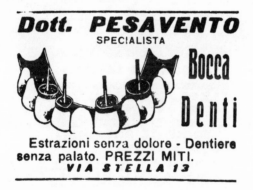

extractions. The pale countenance of the patient under Dr Pesavento did indeed seem perfectly relaxed, but her body twisted and turned in the dentist's chair as if she were undergoing the most agonising discomforts. There were revelations of a different kind, too, such as the pyramid of ten million bottles of Ferro-China table water (to reconstitute the blood), gleaming and glinting in the sun like a promise of eternal

life: a lion roared soundlessly, and soundlessly the pyramid shattered into a myriad little pieces tumbling down slowly in a crystal cascade. They were soundless and weightless, these images and words of times gone by, flaring up briefly and instantly going out, each of them its own empty enigma. The Tyrolese missionary Giuseppe Ohrwalder was reported from Khartoum to have been missing for several weeks at Omdurman in the Sudan. According to telegrams from Danzig, a Colonnello Stern of the 6th Field Artillery Regiment had been arrested there on suspicion of spying: stories with neither beginning nor end, I reflected, which ought to be looked into more closely. 1913 was a peculiar year. The times were changing, and the spark was racing along the fuse like an adder through the grass. Everywhere there were great effusions of feeling. The people were trying out a new role. The sacred and righteous wrath of the nation was invoked. The accounts in the Veronese newspapers of the first festival in the *anfiteatro romano* sought to surpass each other in their enthusiasm. According to one of my notes, an article in the *Fedele* was entitled *Apoteosi dei titani*, in Gothic type. It concluded with the assurance that this headline was no hollow assertion, since the arena was a titanic example of Roman architecture and Giuseppe Verdi the Titan of the *melopoea italiana*. The true Titan of all art and beauty, however, the writer proclaimed with a final flourish, was *il popolo nostro*, and all the rest were nothing but pygmies. For a long time my eyes remained fixed on the six letters of the word *pigmei*, the announcement of a destruction that had already taken place. It was as if I could hear the voice of the people, as it welled up, the violent inflection in the syllables: *pig-me-i, pig-me-i, pig-me-i*. The shouting roared within my ear, in reality doubtless the drumming of my own blood, amplified and distorted by my imagination. At all events, it seemed to prompt no response in the librarian. Calmly he sat bent over his work, filling the lines he had ruled with an even hand. The manner in which he paused at the end of every line suggested that he was writing a list. And plainly he had every detail he needed for the composition of this visibly lengthening register in his head, for he continued his writing without ever referring to any source. Our eyes met on one occasion when he had completed another page and looked up from his work as he reached for the tin that contained the blotting sand. That gesture, which was so out of time, seemed so wholly right at that moment, and so meaningful, that, reassured, I was able to continue my trail through the papers, and as I went on reading and turning the pages, well into the afternoon, I happened on one thing or another that might well be worth retelling some time, such as the report headed UCCISO SUL BANCO ANATOMICO, which began with the truly novelistic words: *Ieri sera nella cella mortuaria de cimitero di Nogara*, and which dealt with the murder of a *carabiniere* named Muzio. The story, which did not lack gruesome details, remained in my memory not least because in one of the tomes I was going through I found an old postcard showing the Cimitero di Staglieno in Genoa. I pocketed the picture and subsequently examined every square inch of it through a magnifying glass. The pale light over the dark hills, the viaduct which appears to lead out of the picture and into a tunnel, the deep shadows near it, the numerous tombs in the shapes of towers or pagodas to the right, the cypress grove, the perspective alignment of the walls, the black field in the foreground, and the white villa at the left end of the main colonnaded walk, all of this, particularly the white villa, seemed so familiar to me that I could easily have found my way around that site blindfolded. In the latter part of the

afternoon I walked along the Adige, beneath the trees of the riverside promenade, to the Castelvecchio. A sandy-coloured dog with a black mark like a patch over its left eye, that appeared like all stray dogs to run at an angle to the direction it was moving in, had attached itself to me outside the duomo, and now kept a steady distance ahead of me. If I paused to gaze down at the river, it paused as well and looked pensively at the flowing water. If I continued on my way, it too went on. But when I crossed the Corso Cavour by the Castelvecchio, it remained on the curb, and when I turned in the middle of the Corso to see where it was I narrowly escaped being run over. Once I was on the other side I wondered whether I should carry straight on through the Via Roma to the Piazza Bra, where I was meeting Salvatore Altamura, or should instead make the short detour through the Via San Silvestro and the Via dei Mutilati. All at once the dog, which had kept its eyes on me from the other side of the Corso, was gone, and so I turned down the Via Roma. I took my time, drifting along with the tide of people in the street, going into this shop and that and at length found myself opposite the Pizzeria Verona, from which I had fled headlong that November evening seven years before. The lettering over Carlo Cadavero's restaurant was still the same, but the entrance was boarded up, and the blinds on the upper floors were drawn, much as I had expected, as I realised in that instant. The image that had lodged in my mind when I fled Verona, and which had recurred time after time, with extreme clarity, before I was at last able to forget it, now presented itself to me again, strangely distorted – two men in black silver-buttoned tunics, who were carrying out from a rear courtyard a bier on which lay, under a floral-patterned drape, what was plainly the body of a human being. Whether this dark apparition was superimposed on reality for a mere moment or for much longer, I could not have said when my senses returned to the daylight and the people, quite unconcerned, passing the pizzeria, which had evidently been shut for some time. When I asked the photographer in the shop next door why the business had closed down, he was unwilling to say anything, nor could I persuade him to photograph the front of the building for me. To my questions and requests he merely responded by shaking his head, as if he did not understand me or was unable to speak. As I was turning to leave, imagining this deaf mute photographer at work in his dark room, I heard him utter a screed of savage curses behind my back, curses which seemed directed less at myself than at some incident which had happened in the restaurant next door. Out on the pavement I wandered irresolutely to and fro before at length I approached a passer-by who seemed suitable for my purpose, a young tourist who came from the Erlangen area, and asked him to take a photograph of the pizzeria for me, which he did, after some hesitation and after I had given him a ten mark note to cover the cost of sending the picture to England in due course. When,

however, I added an urgent request to photograph the flock of pigeons that had just flown from the piazza into the Via Roma, and had settled on the balcony rail and the roof of the building, the young Erlanger, who, as I now thought, might have been on honeymoon, was not prepared to oblige me a second time, probably, I suspected, because his newly-wed bride, who had been eyeing me the whole time with a distrusting and even hostile air and had not budged from his side even when he was taking the picture, was plucking impatiently at his sleeve.

When I arrived at the piazza, Salvatore was already sitting reading outside the bar with the green awning, his glasses pushed up onto his forehead and holding the book so close to his face that it was quite impossible to believe he could decipher anything at all. Taking care not to disturb him, I sat down. The book he was reading had a pink dust jacket bearing the portrait of a woman, in dark colours. Below the portrait, in lieu of a title, were the numbers *1912+1*. A waiter came to the table. He was wearing a long green apron. I ordered a double Fernet on the rocks. Salvatore had meanwhile laid his book aside and restored his glasses to their proper place. He explained apologetically that in the early evening when he had at last escaped the pressures of the daily round he would always turn to a book, even if he had left his reading glasses in the office, as he had today. Once I am at leisure, said Salvatore, I take refuge in prose as one might in a boat. All day long I am surrounded by the clamour on the editorial floor, but in the evening I cross over to an island, and every time, the moment I read the first sentences, it is as if I were rowing far out on the water. It is thanks to my evening reading alone that I am still more or less sane. He was sorry he had not noticed me right away, he said, but being short-sighted and also absorbed in Sciascia's story had cut him off almost completely from what was going on around him. The story Sciascia was telling, he continued, as it were returning to the real world, was a fascinating synopsis of the years immediately before the First World War. At the centre of the narrative, which was more like an essay in form, was one Maria Oggioni *nata* Tiepolo, wife of a Capitano Ferrucio Oggioni, who on the 8th of November, 1912, shot her husband's batman, a *bersagliere* by the name of Quintilio Polimanti, in self-defence according to her own statement. At the time the newspapers naturally made a meal of the story, and the trial, which gripped the nation's imagination for weeks – since after all the accused was of the famous Venetian painter's family, as the press tirelessly repeated – this trial, which kept the entire nation on the edge of its seat, finally revealed no more than a truth familiar to everyone: that the law is not equal for all, and justice not just. Since Polimanti was no longer able to speak for himself, Signora Oggioni, whom everyone was soon calling Contessa Tiepolo, found it easy to win over the judges with that enigmatic smile of hers, a smile that promptly reminded journalists of the Mona Lisa's, as one can imagine, the more so since in 1913 La Gioconda was also in the headlines, having been discovered under the bed of a Florentine workman who had liberated her from her exile in the Louvre two years before and returned her to her native country. It is curious to observe, added Salvatore, how in that year everything was moving towards a single point, at which something would have to happen, whatever the cost. But you, he went on, were interested in a quite different story. And that story, to tell you the end of it first, has now almost reached its conclusion. The trial has been held. The verdict was thirty years. The appeal is due to be heard in Venice in the autumn. I do not think we can expect any new developments. Recently on the phone you said that you were more or less familiar with the story up to the autumn of 1980. The series of ghastly crimes continued after that time. That same autumn in Vicenza, a prostitute by the name of Maria Alice Beretta was killed with a hammer and an axe. Six months later, Luca Martinotti, a grammar school pupil from Verona, succumbed to injuries sustained when an Austrian casemate on the banks of the Etsch, used as a shelter by drug addicts, was torched. In July 1982, two monks, Mario Lovato and Giovanni Pigato, both of advanced years, on their customary walk of an evening round the quiet streets near their monastery, had their skulls smashed in with a heavy-duty hammer. After that killing, a Milan news agency received a letter from the Organizzazione Ludwig, which had already claimed responsibility for the crimes in the autumn of 1980, as you know. If I remember correctly, in the second letter the group claimed that their purpose in life was to destroy those who had betrayed God. In February, the body of a priest, Armando Bison, was found in the Trentino. He lay bludgeoned in his own blood, and a crucifix had been driven into the back of his neck. A further letter proclaimed that the power of Ludwig knew no bounds. In mid-May of the same year, a cinema in Milan, which showed pornographic films, went up in flames. Six men died. Their last picture show bore the title *Lyla, profumo di femmina*. The group claimed responsibility for what they described as a blazing pyre of pricks. In early 1984, on the day after Epiphany, a further arson attack, which also remained unsolved, was made on a discotheque near Munich's main station. It was not until two weeks later that Furlan and

Abel were apprehended. Wearing clowns' costumes, they were carrying open petrol canisters in perforated sports bags through the Melamare disco at Castiglione delle Stiviere, not far from the southern shore of Lake Garda, where that evening four hundred young people had come together for the carnival. It was only by a hair's breadth that the two escaped being lynched by the crowd on the spot. So much for the principal points of the story. Apart from providing irrefutable evidence, the investigation produced nothing that might have made it possible to comprehend a series of crimes extending over almost seven years. Nor did the psychiatric reports afford any real insight into the inner world of the two young men. Both were from highly respected families. Furlan's father is a well-known specialist in burn injuries, and consultant in the plastic surgery department at the hospital here. Abel's father is a retired lawyer, from Germany, who was head of the Verona branch of a Düsseldorf insurance company for years. Both sons went to the Girolamo Fracastro grammar school. Both were highly intelligent. After the school-leaving examinations, Abel went on to study maths and Furlan chemistry. Beyond that, there is little to be said. I think they were like brothers to each other and had no idea how to free themselves from their innocence. I once saw Abel, who was an outstanding guitar player, on a television programme. I think it was in the mid-1970s. He would have been fifteen or sixteen then. And I remember that his whole appearance and his wonderful playing affected me deeply.

Salvatore had come to the end of his account, and night had fallen. Crowds of festival-goers released from their tour buses were gathered outside the arena. The opera, said Salvatore, is not what it used to be. The audience no longer understand that they are part of the occasion. In the old days the carriages used to drive down the long wide road to the Porta Nuova in the evenings, out through the gateway, and westward under the trees along the glacis, skirting the city, till nightfall. Then everyone turned back. Some drove to the churches for the "Ave Maria della Sera", some stopped here on the Bra and the gentlemen stepped up to the carriages to converse with the ladies, often till well into the dark. The days of stepping up to a carriage are over, and the days of the opera also. The festival is a travesty. That is why I cannot bring myself to go into the arena on an evening like this, despite the fact that opera, as you are aware, means a great deal to me. For more than thirty years, said Salvatore, I have been working in this city, and not once have I seen a production in the arena. I sit out here on the Bra, where you cannot hear the music. Neither the orchestra nor the choir nor the soloists. Not a sound. I listen, as it were, to a soundless opera. *La spettacolosa Aida*, a fantastic night on the Nile, as a silent film from the days before the Great War. Did you know, Salvatore continued, that the sets and costumes for the *Aida* being performed in the arena today are exact replicas of those designed by Ettore Fagiuoli and Auguste Mariette for the inauguration of the festival in 1913? One might suppose no time had passed at all, though in fact history is now nearing its close. At times it really does seem to me as if the whole of society were still in the Cairo opera house to celebrate the inexorable advance of Progress. Christmas Eve, 1871. For the first time the strains of the *Aida* overture are heard. With every bar, the incline of the stalls becomes a fraction steeper. The first ship glides through the Suez Canal. On the bridge stands a motionless figure in the white uniform of an admiral, observing the desert through a telescope. You will see the forests again, is Amanoroso's promise. Did you also know that in Scipio's day it was still possible to travel from Egypt to Morocco under the shade of trees? The shade of trees! And now, fire breaks out in the opera house. A crackling conflagration. With a crash the seats in the stalls, together with all their occupants, vanish into the orchestra pit. Through the swathes of smoke beneath the ceiling an unfamiliar figure comes floating down. *Di morte l'angelo a noi s'appressa. Già veggo il ciel discindersi.* But I digress. With these words, Salvatore stood up. You know how I am, he said as he took his leave, when it is getting late. I for my part, however, remained on the piazza for a long time with that image of the descending angel before my eyes. It must have been after midnight, and

the waiter in the green apron had just made his last rounds, when I imagined I heard a horse's hooves on the cobbled square and the sound of carriage wheels; but the carriage itself did not materialise. Instead, there came to my mind pictures of an open-air performance of *Aida* that I had seen in Augsburg as a boy, accompanied by my mother, and of which hitherto I had not had the slightest recollection. The triumphal procession, consisting of a paltry contingent of horsemen and a few sorrow-worn camels and elephants on loan from Circus Krone, as I have recently discovered, passed before me several times, quite as if it had never been forgotten, and, much as it had then in my boyhood, lulled me into a deep sleep from which – though to this day I cannot really explain how – I did not awake till the morning after, in my room at the Golden Dove.

By way of a postscript, I should perhaps add that in April 1924 the writer Franz Werfel visited his friend Franz Kafka

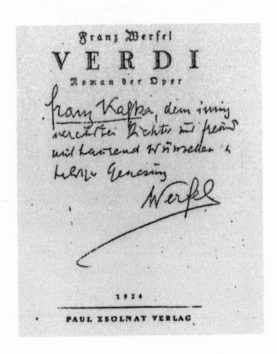

in Hajek's laryngological clinic in Vienna, bearing a bunch of roses and a copy of his newly published and universally acclaimed novel, with a personal dedication. The patient, who at this point weighed a mere 45 kilograms and was shortly to make his final journey to a private nursing home at Klosterneuburg, was probably no longer able to read the book, which may not have been the greatest loss he had to bear. That at least was my own feeling when I leafed

through this operatic tale a few months ago. For me, the only remarkable thing about it was the fact that the copy that had come into my hands, by a circuitous route, had in it the ex libris plate of one Dr Hermann Samson, who must have loved *Aida* so dearly that he had chosen the pyramids, monuments of death, as his insignia.

III

Dr K. Takes the Waters
at Riva

On Saturday the 6th of September, 1913, Dr K., the Deputy Secretary of the Prague Workers' Insurance Company, is on his way to Vienna to attend a congress on rescue services and hygiene. Just as the fate of a man wounded on the battlefield depends upon the quality of the first dressing, he reads in a newspaper he has bought at the border-post of Gmünd, so too the first aid administered at everyday accidents is of the greatest importance for the casualty's recovery. Dr K. finds this statement almost as disquieting as the reference to the social events which will accompany the congress. Outside, Heiligenstadt already: an ominous, deserted station, the trains empty. Dr K. feels he has reached the end of the line and realises that he should have begged the Director on his knees to let him stay in Prague. But of course it is too late now.

In Vienna Dr K. takes a room at the Hotel Matschakerhof, out of sympathy with Grillparzer, who always dined there. It is a gesture of reverence which sadly has no good effect. For most of the time, Dr K. is extremely unwell. He is suffering from dejectedness, and his sight is troubling him. Though he cancels whatever appointments he can, he has a sense of being continually among an alarming number of people. At such times he sits like a ghost at table, suffers bouts of claustrophobia, and imagines that every fleeting glance sees right through him. By his side, close enough to touch, as it were, sits Grillparzer, a man now so ancient that he has almost faded away. He indulges in all sorts of tomfoolery and on one occasion even lays a hand on Dr K.'s knee. During the following night, Dr K. is in a wretched state. His Berlin misadventures are haunting him. He tosses and turns in bed to no avail, puts cold compresses on his head, and stands at the window for a long time gazing down into the street and wishes he lay buried there, a few storeys deeper, in the ground. It is impossible, he notes the following day, to lead the only possible life, to live together with a woman, each one free and independent, married neither in outer appearance nor in reality, to be merely together; and even more impossible to take the only possible step beyond a friendship with men – for there, on the other side of the prescribed boundary, the boot is already upraised that will crush you under its heel.

The most disconcerting part of it, perhaps, is that life nonetheless always goes on, somehow or other. Thus, for instance, in the course of the morning Dr K. is persuaded by Otto Pick to accompany him out to Ottakring to visit Albert Ehrenstein, whose verses he, Dr K., cannot make any sense of, not with the best will in the world. *You, however, take delight in the ship, despoiling the lake with sails. I will go down to the deep. Plunge, thaw, go blind, become ice.* In the tram, Dr K. is suddenly convulsed by a violent aversion to Pick, because the latter has a small, unpleasant hole in his nature through which he sometimes creeps forth in his entirety, as Dr K. now observes. Dr K.'s fretful state of mind is exacerbated when Ehrenstein proves to have a black moustache, exactly like Pick, whom he so resembles he could be his twin brother. As like as two eggs, Dr K. keeps on thinking compulsively. On the way to the Prater he finds the company of the two others increasingly unnerving, and on the gondola pond he feels himself to be a prisoner of their whims. When at last he is returned to dry land, it is small consolation. They might just as well have struck him dead with an oar. Lise Kaznelson, who has also come on the outing, now takes a carousel ride, through the jungle. Dr K. notes how helplessly she sits up there in her billowy, well-cut but ill-worn dress. He experiences a surge of sociable feeling in her presence, as he so often does in the company of women, but otherwise is constantly plagued by one of his headaches. When as a jest they have their photograph taken as passengers in an aeroplane which appears to be flying above the big Ferris wheel and the spires of the Votivkirche, Dr K. is himself bemused to find that he is the only one who can still manage some kind of smile at such dizzy heights. On the 14th of September Dr K. travels

to Trieste. He spends the best part of eight hours on Southern Railways, ensconced in a corner of his compartment. He is seized by a creeping paralysis. Outside the country slips by, in a series of seamlessly changing views, bathed in an altogether improbable autumn light. Although he barely moves a limb, that evening at ten past nine Dr K., incomprehensibly, really is in Trieste. The city lies in darkness. Dr K. is being driven to a harbour-front hotel, and sitting in the horse-drawn hackney-cab, with the broad back of the coachman before him, he has a vision of himself as a most mysterious figure. It seems to him that people are stopping in the street, following him with their eyes, as if to say: there he is at last.

In the hotel he reclines on the bed, hands clasped behind his head, and looks up at the ceiling. Stray cries from outside drift into the room through curtains stirred by a breeze. Dr K. is aware that in this city there is an iron angel who kills travellers from the north, and he longs to go out. On the borderline between grinding weariness and half-sleep he wanders through the lanes of the harbour quarter, sensing under his skin how it is to be a free man waiting on the kerb, hovering an inch above the ground. The circling reflections of the streetlights on the ceiling above him are signs that any moment now it will break open and something will be revealed. Already cracks are appearing in the smooth surface, and then, in a cloud of plaster dust, gradually showing itself against the half-light, a figure descends on great silk-white wings, swathed in bluish-violet vestments and bound with golden cords, the upraised arm with the sword pointing forwards. A veritable angel, thought Dr K. when he could breathe again, all day long it has flown towards me and I of little faith knew nothing of it. Now he will speak to me, he thought, and lowered his gaze. But when he looked up again, the angel, though it was still there, suspended quite low under the ceiling, was no longer a living angel but a garishly painted ship's figurehead, such as hang from the ceilings of sailors' taverns. The sword guard was fashioned to hold candles and catch the dripping tallow.

The next morning Dr K. crossed the Adriatic in somewhat stormy weather, afflicted with slight seasickness. For a considerable time after he had made land, if that is the right expression, in Venice, the waves were still breaking within him. From the Sandwirth Hotel, where he was staying, he wrote to Felice in Berlin, in an optimistic mood that probably came upon him as his queasiness receded, saying that however tremulous he might feel, he now proposed to plunge into the city and all that it could offer a traveller such as himself. Even the pouring rain, which veiled every outline and shape in an even grey-green, would not deter him; no, quite the contrary, he averred, for the days in Vienna would be washed away all the better. However, there is no evidence to suggest that Dr K. did leave the hotel on that 15th of September. If, as he believed, it was impossible to be here at all, how much more was it impossible for him, on the brink of disintegration, to venture out beneath this watery sky under which the very stones dissolved. So Dr K. remains in the hotel. Towards evening, in the sombre lobby, he writes once more to Felice. Now he no longer makes any reference to exploring the city. Instead, set down in hasty lines underneath the hotel's letterhead with its pretty steam yachts, there are references to his mounting despair. That he was alone

and exchanged not a word with a living soul excepting the staff, that the misery within him was almost overflowing, and that – this much he could say with certainty – he was in a condition in keeping with his nature and ordained for him by a justice not of this world, a condition that he could not transcend and which he would have to endure till the very last of his days.

How Dr K. passed his few days in Venice in reality, we do not know. At all events, his sombre mood does not appear to have lifted. Indeed, he felt it was only this state of mind that sustained him when confronted with such a city as Venice, a city which must have made a deep impression upon him, despite there being newly wedded couples everywhere whose very presence seemed to make a mockery of his mournfulness. How it is beautiful, he wrote, with an exclamation mark, in one of those somewhat awry formulations in which language for a moment gives free rein to the emotions. How it is beautiful, and how we undervalue it! But more precise details Dr K. does not disclose. We know, as I have said, nothing of what he really saw. There is not even a reference to the Doge's Palace, the prison chambers of which were to play so prominent a part in the evolution of his own fantasies of trial and punishment some months later. All we know is that he spent those four days in Venice and that he then took the train from Santa Lucia to Verona.

On the afternoon of his arrival in Verona he walked from the station along the Corso into town, and then wandered among its narrow streets until, in weariness, he went into the Church of Sant'Anastasia. After resting in the cool, shadowy interior for a while, with feelings of both gratitude and distaste, he set off once more, and as he left, just as one might ruffle the hair of a son or younger brother, he ran his fingers over the marble locks of a dwarfish figure which, at the foot of one of the mighty columns, had been bearing the immense weight of a holy-water font for centuries. Nowhere is there anything to suggest that he saw the fine mural of St George painted by Pisanello over the entrance to the Pellegrini chapel. It might be shown, though, that when Dr K. stood in the porch once again, on the threshold between the dark interior and the brightness outside, he felt for a moment as if the selfsame church were replicated before him, its entrance fitting directly with that of the church he had just left, a mirroring effect he was familiar with from his dreams, in which everything was forever splitting and multiplying, over and again, in the most terrifying manner.

With the approach of evening, Dr K. began to be aware of the growing numbers of people out on the streets, apparently solely for their pleasure, all of them arm-in-arm in couples or groups of three or even more. Perhaps it was the bills, still posted throughout the city, announcing the *spettacoli lirici all'Arena* that August and the word A I D A displayed in large letters which persuaded him that the Veronese show of carefree togetherness had something of a theatrical performance about it, staged especially to bring home to him, Dr K., his solitary, eccentric condition – a thought he could not get out of his head and which he was only able to escape by seeking refuge in a cinema, probably the Cinema Pathé di San Sebastiano. In tears, so Dr K. recorded the following day in Desenzano, he sat in the surrounding darkness, observing the transformation into pictures of the minute particles of dust glinting in the beam of the projector. However, there is nothing in Dr K.'s Desenzano notes to tell us of what he saw on that 20th of September in Verona. Was it the Pathé newsreel, featuring the review of the cavalry in the presence of His Majesty Vittorio Emanuele III, and *La Lezione dell'abisso*, which, as I discovered in the Biblioteca Civica, were shown that day at the Pathé and which are both now untraceable? Or was it, as I initially supposed, a story that ran with some success in the cinemas of Austria in 1913, the story of the unfortunate Student of Prague, who cut himself off from love and life when, on the 13th of May, 1820, he sold his soul to a certain Scapinelli? The extraordinary exterior shots in this film, the silhouettes of his native city flickering across the screen, would doubtless have sufficed to move Dr K. deeply, most of all perhaps the fate of the eponymous hero, Balduin, since in him he would have recognised a kind of *doppelgänger*, just as Balduin recognises his other self in the dark-coated brother whom he could never and nowhere escape. In one of the very first scenes, Balduin, the finest swordsman in all Prague, confronts his own image in the mirror, and presently, to his horror, that unreal figure steps out of the frame, and

henceforth follows him as the ghostly shadow of his own restlessness. Would this sort of scenario not have struck Dr K. as the description of a struggle in which, as in the contest he himself had set against the backdrop of the Laurenziberg, the principal character and his opponent are in the most intimate and self-destructive of relationships, such that, when the hero is driven into a corner by his companion he is forced to declare: I am betrothed, I admit it. And what alternative does a man so cornered have but to try and rid himself of his dumb attendant by means of a shot from a pistol? – a shot which, in the silent film, is visible as a puff of smoke. In that moment, in which time itself seems to dissolve, Balduin is released from his delusions. He breathes freely once more and, realising in the same instant that the bullet has penetrated his own heart, dies a dramatic, not to say ostentatious death, the whole scene like a flickering light about to be extinguished, representing the soundless aria of the hero's demise. Final contortions of this kind, which regularly occur in opera when, as Dr K. once wrote, the dying voice aimlessly wanders through the music, did not by any means seem ridiculous to him; rather he believed them to be an expression of our, so to speak, natural misfortune, since after all, as he remarks elsewhere, we lie prostrate on the boards, dying, our whole lives long.

On the 21st of September Dr K. is in Desenzano on the southern shore of Lake Garda. Most of the townspeople have gathered in the market square to welcome the Deputy Secretary of the Prague Workers' Insurance Company. Dr K.,

however, is reclining on the grass down by the lake, before him the waves lapping the reeds, to his right the promontory of Sirmione, to his left the shore towards Manerba. Simply to lie in the grass is one of Dr K.'s favourite ways of passing the time, when reasonably well disposed. If at such a moment, as once happened in Prague, a gentleman of some distinction with whom he has occasionally had official dealings rides by in a two-horse carriage, Dr K. relishes the pleasures (but only, as he notes himself, the pleasures) of being declassed and freed from all social standing. In Desenzano, however, even this modest happiness eludes him. Rather he feels ill, sick, as he puts it, at every point of the compass. There remains only the one consolation that nobody knows where he is. We have no record of how long the people of Desenzano continued their watch for the Deputy Secretary from Prague that afternoon, nor when, disappointed, they finally dispersed.

One of them is reported to have observed that those in whom we invest our hopes only ever make their appearance when they are no longer needed.

Following this failed encounter, which was as disheartening for him as it was for the people of Desenzano, Dr K.

spends three weeks in Riva at Dr von Hartungen's hydropathic establishment, arriving by steamer just before nightfall that day. A porter wearing a long green apron fastened at the back with a brass chain shows Dr K. to his room, from the balcony of which he gazes out over the lake, serenely peaceful in the gathering darkness. All is now blue on blue, and nothing appears to move, not even the steamer, already some way out upon the water. In the morning, the daily routine of the hydro begins. In the intervals between the various cold douches and the electrical treatment prescribed for him, Dr K. tries as far as possible to immerse himself entirely in quiet and tranquillity, but the woes he endured with Felice, and she with him, continually come over him, like a living thing, usually when he

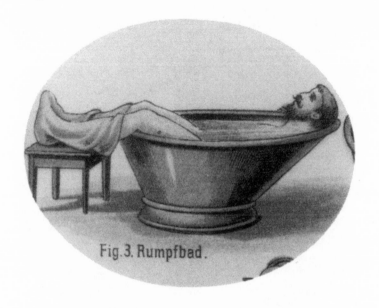

Fig. 3. Rumpfbad.

awakes, though also at mealtimes when he often feels quite paralysed and unable to pick up his knife and fork. At table, as it happens, the place to Dr K.'s right is occupied by an old general who remains silent for the most part, but now and then will venture a cryptic yet penetrating observation. Thus on one occasion, looking up abruptly from the book which always lies open beside him, he remarks that, when one thinks about it, a vast range of unfathomable contingencies come between the logic of the battleplan and that of the final despatches, both of which he knew inside out. Tiny details imperceptible to us decide everything! Even the greatest battles in the history of the world were won or

Dr K. Takes the Waters at Riva

lost like that. Tiny details, but they weigh as heavy as the 50,000 dead soldiers and horses at Waterloo. The fact is that ultimately it all comes down to the question of specific gravity. Stendhal had a clearer grasp of this than any high command, he says, and now, in my old age, I have apprenticed myself to that old master, so that I may not die quite without understanding. It is a fundamentally insane notion, he continues, that one is able to influence the course of events by a turn of the helm, by will-power alone, whereas in fact all is determined by the most complex interdependencies.

Although he is aware that the remarks of his dining companion are not directed at himself, Dr K. experiences a slight surge of confidence and a species of tacit solidarity as he listens. The girl to his left, whom he takes to be unhappy on account of the silent gentleman to her right, that is, on account of himself, now begins interestingly to acquire definition in his mind. She is somewhat short of stature, comes from Genoa, looks very Italian, but is in fact from Switzerland, and, it now transpires, has a voice of a curiously dark timbre. Whenever she speaks to him in that voice, an infrequent enough occurrence, it seems to Dr K. like an extraordinary expression of confidence and trust. In her frail condition she becomes most precious to him, and before long he is rowing out a short way onto the lake with her

157

in the afternoons. The crags rise from the water in the mellow autumn light, nuanced in shades of green, as if the entire location were an album and the mountains had been drawn on an empty page by some sensitive dilettante, as a remembrance for the lady to whom the album belongs.

Out there they tell each other their ailments, both of them, as one would like to believe, buoyed up by an ephemeral improvement in their condition and sense of peaceable quiescence. Dr K. evolves a fragmentary theory of disembodied love, in which there is no difference between intimacy and disengagement. If only we were to open our eyes, he says, we would see that our happiness lies in our natural surroundings and not in our poor bodies which have long since become separated from the natural order of things. That was the reason why all false lovers (and all lovers, he adds, are false) closed their eyes while lovemaking or else, which came to the same thing, kept them wide open with craving. Never were we more helpless or lacking in rational sense than in that condition. Our dreams could then be constrained no longer and we became subject to the compulsion of constantly going through the whole gamut of variations and repetitions which, as he himself had often enough found, extinguished everything, even the image of the lover one so wished to preserve. Curiously, when he became caught up in such states, which he considered bordered on madness, the only thing that helped was to clap an imaginary black Napoleonic tricorne over his thoughts. At present, however, there was nothing he had less need of than such a hat, for out here on the lake they were indeed almost disembodied, and possessed of a natural understanding of their own scant significance.

In accordance with the expressed hopes of Dr K., they agreed that neither would divulge the other's name, that they would exchange no pictures, nor a shred of paper, nor even a single written word, and that once the few days that remained to them were over they must simply let each other go. In the event though it was not easy. When the hour of their parting arrived, Dr K. had to create all manner of comical diversions to prevent the girl from Genoa from sobbing in front of the leave-taking party. When at last Dr K. accompanied her down to the steamer jetty, and she mounted the little gangplank to board the ship, with an unsteady step, he recalled how a few evenings previously they had joined some other residents and a young, extremely wealthy, very elegant Russian woman had told their fortunes from the cards, out of boredom and desperation – for elegant persons are more often alone among the unstylish than vice versa. Nothing of any consequence emerged out of this purely frivolous and foolish charade. Not until it was the turn of the girl from Genoa did an unambiguous constellation come up, which caused the Russian lady to inform her that she would never enter the so-called state of matrimony. For Dr K. it was uncanny in the extreme to hear a solitary life foretold from the cards for this girl of all people, the object of his affections, whom he had thought of as the mermaid ever since he had first seen her, on account of her water-green eyes; for there was nothing of a spinster about her at all, except perhaps the way she wore her hair, as he now thought to himself on seeing her for the last time, her right hand on the rail, while the left described, somewhat awkwardly, a sign in the air which betokened the end.

The steamer cast off and, sounding its horn a number of times, slipped out onto the lake at an oblique angle. Undine was still standing at the rail. After a while he could barely distinguish her outline, and then the ship itself had become almost invisible. Only the white wake which it trailed through the water was still to be seen until this was also smoothed over. As for the tarot cards, Dr K., walking back to the sanatorium, had to acknowledge that in his own case too they had resulted in quite unequivocal constellations, inasmuch as all the cards which showed not merely numbers but kings, queens and knaves were, invariably, as far as possible removed from his person, to the very limits of the game, so to speak. Indeed, on one occasion when the cards were laid, only two figures appeared at all, and another time none whatsoever, evidently a most unusual distribution and one which prompted the Russian lady to look upwards into his eyes and declare that he must surely be the strangest guest in Riva in a long time.

In the early afternoon of the day following the mermaid's departure, Dr K. lay resting as the establishment's rules required when he heard hurried footsteps in the corridor outside his room, and the customary silence had hardly returned than they were heard again, this time going in the other direction. When Dr K. looked out into the passage, to see what had occasioned this to-ing and fro-ing in breach of all the hydro's practices, he glimpsed Dr von Hartungen, his white coat flying and attended by two nurses, just turning the corner. Later that afternoon the mood in all of the reception rooms was curiously subdued, and at tea the staff were noticeably monosyllabic. The sanatorium patients exchanged glances in embarrassed consternation, like children forbidden to speak by their parents. At dinner, Dr K.'s right-hand table companion, retired General of Hussars Ludwig von Koch, whom he had come to look upon as an amiable permanent fixture and to whom he had hoped to turn for consolation after the loss of the girl from Genoa, was not in his place. Dr K. now had no neighbour at table at all, and sat quite alone at dinner, like a man with a contagious disease. The next morning the sanatorium management announced that Major General Ludwig von Koch, of Neusiedl in Hungary, had passed away in the early afternoon of the previous day. In answer to his concerned enquiries, Dr K. learned from Dr von Hartungen that General von Koch had taken his own life, with his old army pistol. In some incomprehensible way, Dr von Hartungen added with a nervous gesture, he had contrived to shoot himself both in the heart and in the head. He was found in his armchair, the novel he had always been reading lying open in his lap.

The funeral, which took place on the 6th of October in Riva, was a desolate affair. It had not proved possible to notify the only relative of the General, who had neither wife nor children. Dr von Hartungen, one of the nurses, and Dr K. were the only mourners. The priest, reluctant to bury a suicide, performed the office in the most cursory manner. The funeral oration was confined to an appeal to the Almighty Father in his infinite goodness to grant everlasting peace to this taciturn and oppressed soul – *quest'uomo più taciturno e mesto*, said the priest, his gaze upturned with a reproachful expression. Dr K. seconded this meagre wish and, once the ceremony had been concluded with a few more mumbled words, he followed Dr von Hartungen, at some distance, back to the sanatorium. The October sun shone so warm that day that Dr K. was obliged to take off his hat and carry it in his hand.

Over the years that followed, lengthy shadows fell upon those autumn days at Riva, which, as Dr K. on occasion said to himself, had been so beautiful and so appalling, and from these shadows there gradually emerged the silhouette of a barque with masts of an inconceivable height and sails dark

and hanging in folds. Three whole years it takes until the
vessel, as if it were being borne across the waters, gently
drifts into the little port of Riva. It berths in the early hours
of the morning. A man in blue overalls comes ashore and
makes fast the ropes. Behind the boatmen, two figures in
dark tunics with silver buttons carry a bier upon which lies,
under a large floral-patterned cover, what was clearly the
body of a human being. It is Gracchus the huntsman. His
arrival was announced at midnight to Salvatore, the *podestà*
of Riva, by a pigeon the size of a cockerel, which flew in at
his bedroom window and then spoke in his ear. Tomorrow,
the pigeon said, the dead hunter Gracchus will arrive. Receive
him in the name of the town. After some deliberation,
Salvatore arose and set the necessary preparations in train.
Now, entering the lord mayor's office in the light of dawn, his
cane and top hat with its mourning band in his black-gloved
right hand, he finds to his satisfaction that his instructions
have been followed correctly. Fifty boys forming a guard of
honour stand in the long hallway, and in one of the rear
rooms on the upper storey, as he hears from the ship's master,
who meets him at the entrance, Gracchus the huntsman lies
upon his bier, a man, it now transpires, of wild, tangled hair
and beard, his ravaged skin darkened to the colour of bronze.
   We the readers, the sole witnesses of what was said between

the huntsman and the deputy of the community of Riva, learn little of the fate of Gracchus, except that many, many years before, in the Black Forest, where he was on guard against the wolves which still prowled the hills at that time, he went in pursuit of a chamois – and is this not one of the strangest items of misinformation in all the tales that have ever been told? – he went in pursuit of a chamois and fell to his death from the face of a mountain; and that because of a wrong turn of the tiller, a moment of inattention on the part of the helmsman, distracted by the beauty of the huntsman's dark green country, the barque which was to have ferried him to the shore beyond failed to make the crossing, so that he, Gracchus, has been voyaging the seas of the world ever since, without respite, as he says, attempting now here and now there to make land. The question of who is to blame for this undoubtedly great misfortune remains unresolved, as indeed does the matter of what his guilt, the cause of his misfortune, consists in. But as it was Dr K. who conjured up this tale, it seems to me that the meaning of Gracchus the huntsman's ceaseless journey lies in a penitence for a longing for love, such as invariably besets Dr K., as he explains in one of his countless *Fledermaus*-letters to Felice, precisely at the point where there is seemingly, and in the natural and lawful order of things, nothing to be enjoyed.

The better to elucidate this somewhat impenetrable observation, Dr K. adduces an episode from "the evening before last", in which the son – now surely aged forty – of the owner of a Jewish bookshop in Prague becomes the focus of the illicit emotion described in this letter. This man, in no way attractive, indeed repulsive, who has had almost nothing but misfortune in life, spends the entire day in his father's tiny store, dusting off the prayer stoles or peeking out at the street through gaps between books which, Dr K. expressly notes, are mostly of an obscene nature; this wretched creature, who feels himself (as Dr K. knows) to be German and for that reason goes to the Deutsches Haus every evening after supper to nurture his delusion of grandeur as a member of the German Casino Club, becomes for Dr K., in that episode which occurred the day before yesterday, as he tells Felice, an object of fascinated interest in a way he cannot entirely explain even to himself. Quite by chance, writes Dr K., I noticed him leaving the shop yesterday evening. He walked ahead of me, every inch the young man I had in my memory. His back is strikingly broad, and he bears himself so curiously upright that it is hard to tell whether he is indeed straight as a ramrod or malformed. Do you now understand, my dearest, writes Dr K., can you understand (*please tell me!*) why it was that I followed this man down Zeltnergasse, veritably lusting, turned into the Graben behind him, and watched him enter the gates of the Deutsches Haus with a feeling of unbounded pleasure?

At this point Dr K. surely came within an inch of admitting to a desire which we must assume remained unstilled. But instead, remarking that it is already late, he hastily concludes his letter, one which he had begun with comments on a photograph of a niece of Felice's, writing: Yes, this little child deserves to be loved. That fearful gaze, as if all the terrors of the earth had been revealed to her in the studio. But what love could have been sufficient to spare the child the terrors of love, which for Dr K. stood foremost among all the terrors of the earth? And how are we to fend off the fate of being unable to depart this life, lying before the *podestà*, confined to a bed in our sickness, and, as Gracchus the huntsman does, touching, in a moment of distraction, the knee of the man who was to have been our salvation.

IV

Il ritorno in patria

In November 1987, after spending the last weeks of the summer in Verona, working on my various tasks, and the month of October, because I could not bear to wait any longer for the onset of winter, in a hotel high above Bruneck, near the tree line, I decided one afternoon, when the Großvenediger emerged from behind a grey snow cloud in an especially ominous way, that I should return to England, but before that go to W. for a while, where I had not been since my childhood. As there was only one bus a day from Innsbruck to Schattwald, and that, as far as I could discover, at seven in the morning, I had no alternative but to take the night express across the Brenner, a train with unpleasant associations for me, which arrives in Innsbruck at about half past four. At Innsbruck, as always when I arrive there, no matter what the time of year, the weather was quite atrocious. It cannot have been more than five or six degrees above zero, and the clouds were hanging so low that the tops of the houses disappeared in them and the dawn could not break through. Moreover, it rained incessantly. So there was no question of walking into town or taking a stroll along the river Inn. I looked out across the deserted station forecourt. Now and then some vehicle would crawl slowly along the gleaming black roads, the last of an amphibian species close to extinction, retreating now to the deeper waters. The ticket hall was also deserted, apart from a small chap with a goitre wearing a green loden cape. Holding his folded, dripping umbrella against his shoulder with its tip upwards like a rifle, he was walking back and forth with measured tread and making such precise about-turns that he might have been guarding the Tomb of the Unknown Soldier. The down-and-outs then appeared, one after the other, though from where was uncertain, till there were a dozen of them, a lively group gathered around a crate of Gösser beer which had made a sudden miraculous appearance in their midst, seemingly out of thin air. United by the inveterate alcoholism of the Tyrol which is known for its extremism far beyond the region, these Innsbruck dossers, some of whom appeared to have only recently dropped out of ordered life, while others were already in a completely ruinous state, and every single one of whom had something of the philosopher or even of the preacher about him, were holding forth on current events as well as the most fundamental questions. It was remarkable in their disputations that those who chimed in at the top of their voices were invariably the ones who left off in mid-sentence, suddenly silenced as if by a stroke. Whatever happened to be the topic, every point was underscored by highly theatrical, apodictic gestures, and even when one of their number, no longer able to put into words the thought which had just come into his head, turned away with a wave of contempt, it seemed to me as if their manner derived from a distinctive dramatic repertoire completely unknown on the stage. Possibly this was because all of them were holding their beer bottles in their right hands, and were thus in a sense acting out one-armed, left-handed roles. And perhaps, I concluded from this observation, it might be a good ploy to tie the right hands of all drama students behind their backs for a year at the start of their training. With reflections such as these I passed the time until increasing numbers of commuters began traversing the hall, and the dossers made themselves scarce. At six o'clock on the dot, the so-called Tiroler Stuben opened, and I took a seat in a restaurant which for sheer dreariness far surpassed every other station bar I had ever been in, ordered a coffee and leafed through the *Tiroler Nachrichten*. Neither of these, the Tyrolean morning coffee nor the *Tiroler Nachrichten*, did anything to improve my state of mind. It therefore did not surprise me in the slightest when things took an even worse turn, and the waitress, to whom I had made a joking remark about the corrosive properties of the Tyrolean chicory coffee, gave me the benefit of her sharp tongue in the most ill-tempered manner imaginable.

Frozen through and bleary-eyed from lack of sleep as I was, the insolence of this Innsbruck waitress like a noxious poison went right under my skin. The words in the news-paper jittered and swam before my eyes, and more than once I felt as though my insides had seized up. Not until the bus was leaving town did I gradually begin to feel somewhat better. It was still pouring with rain, so heavily that the houses close to the road could hardly be made out, and the mountains not at all. Now and then the bus stopped so that one of the old women standing at intervals along the roadside beneath their black umbrellas could get on. Soon quite a number of these Tyrolean women were aboard. In the dialect I was familiar with from childhood, croakily articulated at the back of the throat like some bird

language, they talked mainly or indeed exclusively about the
never-ending rain, which in many places had already caused
whole mountainsides to slide into the valleys. They spoke of
the hay rotting in the fields and the potatoes rotting in the
ground; of the redcurrants which had come to nothing for
a third year in a row; of the elder, which this year had not
flowered until the beginning of August and had then been
completely ruined by the rain; and of the fact that not a
single eatable apple had been picked far and wide. As they
went on discussing the effects of the ever-worsening weather,
complaining that there was neither sunlight nor warmth,
the scene outside brightened up, a little at first and then
more and more. One could now see the river Inn, its waters
meandering through broad stony reaches, and soon beautiful
green meadows came into view. The sun came out, the
entire landscape was radiant, and the Tyrolean women fell
silent one after the other and simply looked out at the miracle
passing by. I felt much the same myself. The countryside
seemed freshly varnished – we were now driving out of the
Inn valley in the direction of the Fern Pass – and the steaming
forests and blue skies above, though I had come up from the
south and had had to endure the Tyrolean darkness for only
a couple of hours, were like a revelation even to me. Once
I noticed a dozen hens right out in the middle of a green

field. For some reason that I still cannot fathom, the sight of this small flock that had ventured so far out into the open affected me deeply. I do not know what it is about certain things or creatures that sometimes moves me like this. The road climbed steadily upwards. The flame-red stands of larch trees were blazing on the sides of the mountains, and I saw that snow had fallen a long way down. We crossed the Fern Pass. I marvelled at the screes which reached from the mountains down into the forests like pale fingers into dark hair, and I was astonished again at the mysterious slow motion quality of the water-falls which, for as long as I could remember, had been cascading, unchanged, over the rock faces. At a hairpin bend I looked out of the turning bus down into the depths below and could see the turquoise surfaces of the Fernstein and Samaranger lakes, which, even when I was a child, on our first excursions into the Tyrol, had seemed to me the essence of all conceivable beauty.

Around noon – the Tyrolean women had long since got out at Reutte, Weißenbach, Haller, Tannheim and Schattwald – the bus, with me as its last passenger, reached the Oberjoch customs post. Meanwhile, the weather had changed once again. A dark layer of cloud, verging on the black, lay across the entire Tannheim valley, which made a lightless and godforsaken impression. There was not the slightest sign of movement anywhere. Not even a single car could be seen on the stretch of road disappearing far into the remoter depths of the valley. On one side the mountains rose up into the mists; on the other lay wet boggy grassland, and behind it, from out of the Vilsgrund, arose the wedge of the Pfronten forests, consisting solely of blackish-blue spruce. The customs officer on duty, who told me he lived in Maria Rain, promised to drop off my bag at the Engelwirt inn when he finished work, on his way home through W., which left me free, once I had exchanged a few generalities with him about the dreadfulness of this time of year, to set off carrying nothing but my small leather rucksack over my shoulder, through the boggy meadows bordering the no man's land and down through the Alpsteig gorge to Krummenbach, and from there to Unterjoch, past the Pfeiffermühle and through the Enge Plätt to W. The gorge was sunk in a darkness that I would not have thought possible in the middle of the day. Only, to my left, above the brook invisible from the path, there hung a little meagre light. Spruce trees, a good seventy to eighty years old, stood on the slopes. Even on those growing up from the depths of the ravine, the evergreen tops did not appear until far above the level of the path. Time and again, whenever there was a movement in the air above, the drops of water caught in the countless pine needles came raining down. In places where the spruce stood further apart, grew isolated beech trees that had long since shed their leaves, their branches and trunks blackened by the persistent wet. It was quite still in the gorge save for the sound of the water at the bottom, no birdsong, nothing. Increasingly a sense of trepidation oppressed me, and it seemed as if the further down I walked, the colder and gloomier it became. At one of the few more open places, where a vantage-point afforded a view both down onto a waterfall and a deep rockpool and upwards into the sky, without my being able to say which was the more eerie, I saw through the apparently infinite loftiness of the trees, flurries of snow high up in the leaden greyness, but none of it had yet found its way down into the gorge. After a further half-hour's walk, when the gorge opened out and the meadows of Krummenbach lay before me, I stopped for a long time beneath the last trees, watching from out of the darkness as the whitish-grey snow fell, its silence completely extinguishing what little pallid colour there was in those wet deserted fields. Not far from the margin of the forest stands the Krummenbach chapel, so small that it can surely not have been possible for more than a dozen to attend a service or worship there at the same time. In that walled cell I sat for a while. Outside, snowflakes were drifting past the small window, and presently it seemed to me as if I were in a boat on a voyage, crossing vast waters. The moist smell of lime became sea air; I could feel the spray on my forehead and the boards swaying beneath my feet, and I imagined myself sailing in this ship out of the flooded mountains. But what I remember most about the Krummenbach chapel, apart from this transformation of the stone walls into the hull of a wooden boat, is the Stations of the Cross, painted by some unskilled hand around the mid-eighteenth century, and half already covered and eaten by mould. Even on the somewhat better preserved scenes, little could be made out with any degree of certainty – faces distorted in pain and anger, dislocated limbs, an arm raised to strike. The garments, painted in dark colours, had merged beyond recognition with the background, which was equally unrecognisable. Insofar as anything was still visible at all, it was like looking at some ghostly battle of faces and hands suspended in the gloom of decay. I could not then and cannot now recall whether I was ever in the Krummenbach chapel as a child with my grandfather, who took me with him everywhere. But there were many chapels like that of Krummenbach around W., and much of what I saw and felt in them at the time will have stayed with me – a fear of the acts of cruelty depicted there no less than the wish, in all its impossibility, that the perfect tranquillity prevailing within them might sometime be recaptured. When the snow had eased off, I started on my way again, through the Bränte and along the Krummenbach as far as Unterjoch, where I ate bread soup and drank half a litre of Tyrolean wine at the Hirschwirt inn, to warm myself and prepare for the next stretch, which would be twice the distance. Perhaps prompted by the pitiful pictures in the Krummenbach chapel, my mind turned to Tiepolo once again, and the belief I had held for a long time that, when he travelled with his sons Lorenzo and Domenico from Venice across the Brenner in the autumn of 1750, he decided at Zirl that, contrary to the advice he had been given to leave the Tyrol via Seefeld, he instead made his way westward via Telfs, following the salt wagons across the Gaicht Pass, through the Tannheim valley, over the Oberjoch and through the Iller valley into the lowlands. And I beheld Tiepolo, who must have been approaching sixty by that time and already suffered badly from gout, lying in the cold of the winter months at the top of the scaffolding half a metre below the ceiling of the grand stairway in the palace at Würzburg, his face splattered with lime and distemper, applying the colours with a steady hand, despite the pain in his right arm, onto the wet plaster of the immense, miraculous painting he was creating little by little. With imaginings such as these, and thinking about the Krummenbach painter who had, perhaps in the very same winter, toiled just as hard to represent the fourteen small Stations of the Cross as Tiepolo with his magnificent fresco, I walked on, the time being now about three o'clock, through the fields below the Sorgschrofen and the Sorgalpe, till I struck the road shortly before reaching the Pfeiffermühle. From there it was another hour to W. The last of the daylight was fading by the time I got to the Enge Plätt. To my left was the river, to the right the dripping rock faces through which the road had been blasted at the turn of the century. Above, in front and presently behind me there was nothing but the unstirring black pine forests. The last stretch of the journey was as never-ending as I remembered it from the old days. In the Enge Plätt in April 1945, a so-called last skirmish took place, in which, as it says on the iron memorial cross which still stands in the cemetery in W., 24-year-old Alois Thimet of Rosenheim, 41-year-old Erich Daimler of Stuttgart, 17-year-old Rudolf Leitenstorfer (place of birth unknown), and Werner Hempel (year of birth unknown) of Börneke, died for their Fatherland. In the course of my childhood in W. I heard people speak of that last skirmish on various occasions,

and imagined the combatants with soot-blackened faces, crouching behind tree trunks with their rifles at the ready or leaping from rock to rock across the deepest chasms, suspended motionless in mid-air, for at least as long as I could hold my breath or keep my eyes shut.

It was dusk by the time I had passed through the Plätt. White mists were rising from the meadows, and below, by the river, now a good distance away, stood the black sawmill, which, together with its timberyard, burned to the ground in the 1950s, a few days after I started school, in a huge fire that lit up the whole of the valley. Darkness now descended on the road. In former times, when it was made up with crushed limestone, it had been easier to walk on, I remembered, and almost the colour of white. Like a luminous ribbon, it had stretched out before one even on a starless night, I recalled, realising at the same time that I could scarcely lift my feet for weariness. Also, it seemed strange that not a single vehicle had overtaken me, or had come from the other direction, on the whole stretch from the Unterjoch. I stood for a long time on the stone bridge a short distance before the first houses of W., listening to the steady murmur of the river and looking into the blackness which now enveloped everything. On a piece of waste land beside the bridge, where willows, deadly nightshade, burdock, mulleins, verbena and mugwort used to grow, there had always been a gypsy camp in the summer months after the war. Whenever we went to the swimming pool, which the council had built in 1936 to promote public health, we would pass the gypsies, and every time as we did so my mother picked me up and carried me in her arms. Across her shoulder I saw the gypsies look up briefly from what they were about, and then lower their eyes again as if in revulsion.

I do not believe that any of the locals ever spoke to them, nor as far as I know did the gypsies come into the village to hawk goods or tell fortunes. Where they came from, how they had managed to survive the war, and why of all places they had chosen that cheerless spot by the Ach bridge for their summer camp, are questions that occur to me only now – for example, when I leaf through the photo album which my father bought as a present for my mother for the first so-called Kriegsweihnacht. In it are pictures of the Polish campaign, all neatly captioned in white ink. Some of these photographs show gypsies who had been rounded up and put in detention. They are looking out, smiling, from behind the barbed wire, somewhere in a far corner of the

Slovakia where my father and his vehicle repairs unit had been stationed for several weeks before the outbreak of war.

A good thirty years had gone by since I had last been in W. In the course of that time – by far the longest period of my life – many of the localities I associated with it, such as the Altachmoos, the parish woods, the tree-lined lane that led to Haslach, the pumping station, Petersthal cemetery where the plague dead lay, or the house in the Schray where Dopfer the hunchback lived, had continually returned in my dreams and daydreams and had become more real to me than they had been then, yet the village itself, I reflected, as I arrived at that late hour, was more remote from me than any other place I could conceive of. In a certain sense it was reassuring, on my first walk around the streets in the pale glow of the lamps, to find that everything was completely changed. The house of the head forester, a small shingled villa with a pair of antlers and the inscription "1913" above the front door, together with its small orchard, had made way for a holiday home; the fire station and its handsome slatted tower, where the fire brigade's hoses hung in silent anticipation of the next conflagration, were no longer there; the farmhouses had without exception been rebuilt, with added storeys; the vicarage, the curate's lodge, the school, the town hall where Fürgut the one-armed clerk went in and out of with a regularity that my grandfather could set his watch by, the cheese dairy, the poorhouse, Michael Meyer's grocery and haberdashery – all had been thoroughly modernised or had disappeared altogether. Not even when I entered the Engelwirt inn did I have any sense of knowing my way around, for here too, where we had lived in rented accommodation on the first floor for several years, the whole house had been rebuilt and converted from the foundations up to the very rafters, not to mention the changes to the furnishings and fittings. What now presented itself, in the pseudo-Alpine style which has become the new vernacular throughout the Federal Republic, as a house offering refined hospitality to its patrons, in those distant days was a hostelry of disrepute where the village peasants sat around until deep into the night and, particularly in winter, often drank themselves senseless. The Engelwirt inn owed its local standing, which remained unassailable despite everything, to the fact that, in addition to the smoke-filled bar beneath the ceiling of which ran the longest and most crooked stove-pipe I have ever seen, it had a large function room in which long tables could be set up for weddings and funerals, with enough seating for half the village. Every fortnight the newsreel would be shown there and feature films such as *Piratenliebe, Niccolò Paganini, Tomahawk* and

Mönche, Mädchen und Panduren. The cavalry irregulars referred to in this this last title could be seen charging through dappled birch woods; Indians rode across limitless plains; the crippled violinist reeled off a cadenza at the base of a prison wall while his companion filed through the iron bars of his cell window; General Eisenhower, on his return from Korea, got out of an aeroplane, the propeller of which was still revolving slowly; a hunter whose chest had been torn open by a bear's paw staggered down into the valley; politicians were seen in front of the new parliament, ' climbing out of the back of a Volkswagen; and almost every week we saw the mountains of rubble in places like Berlin or Hamburg, which for a long time I did not associate with the destruction wrought in the closing years of the war, knowing nothing of it, but considered them a natural condition of all larger cities. Of all the events ever put on in the Engelwirt function room, it was an amateur production of Schiller's *The Robbers*, staged there several times during the winter of 1948 or 1949 which made the greatest impression on me. Half a dozen times, at least, I must have sat in the darkened Engelwirt hall among an audience some of whom had come over from neighbouring villages. Scarcely ever has anything that I have seen in the theatre since affected me as much as the *The Robbers* – Old Moor in the ice-cold exile

187

of his bleak house, the gruesome Franz with his deformed shoulder, the return of the prodigal son from the forests of Bohemia, or that curious slight movement of the body, never failing to excite me, with which the deathly pale Amalia said: *Hark, hark! Did I not hear the gate?* And there, before her, is Moor the robber, and she speaks of how her love made the burning sand green and the thorn bushes blossom, without ever knowing that the man from whom she still supposed herself to be separated by mountains, oceans and horizons had come home and was standing beside her. Always then I would wish to intervene in the proceedings and in a single word tell Amalia that she had only to reach out her hand in order to move from her dusty prison to that paradise of love she so desired. But since I could not bring myself to call out in this way, the turn that the events might otherwise have taken was never revealed to me. Towards the end of the play's run, in early February, it was given an open-air performance, in the paddock next to the postmaster's house, mainly, I suppose, so that a series of photographs could be taken. The winter's tale that resulted was notable not only on account of the snow which covered the ground in this open-air production even in the scenes set indoors, but mainly because Moor the robber now entered the action on horseback, which had of course not been possible in the function room. I believe it was on this occasion that I first noticed that horses often have a

somewhat crazed look in their eyes. At all events, that performance on the postmaster's paddock was the last of *The Robbers*, and indeed the last theatre performance of any kind in W. Only during carnival time did the actors don their costumes once more, to join the carnival procession and take their places in a group photograph together with the fire brigade and the clowns.

Behind the reception desk in the Engelwirt, after I had rung the bell several times to no avail, a tight-lipped woman eventually materialised. I had not heard a door open anywhere, not seen her come in, and yet there she suddenly was. She scrutinised me with open disapproval, perhaps on account of my outward appearance, which was none the better for my long walk, or because I betrayed an absent-mindedness that must have been unaccountable to her. I asked for a room on the first floor facing on to the street, initially for an indefinite period. Although it must have been possible to comply readily with my request, since November, in the hotel trade too, is the month of the dead, during which time the reduced service staff in the now vacant houses mourn the departed guests as if they had taken leave for ever – although a room on the first floor facing on to the street must without doubt have been available, the receptionist endlessly leafed back and forth in her register before handing the keys to me. She held her cardigan together with her left hand, as if she were cold, awkwardly and clumsily performing her tasks using only her other hand, so that it seemed to me as if she were marking time in order to make up her mind about this odd November guest. She studied the completed registration form, on which I had given "foreign correspondent" as my occupation and written my complicated English address, with raised eyebrows, for when and for what purpose had an English foreign correspondent ever come to W., on foot, in November, and unshaven to boot, and taken a room in the Engelwirt inn for an indefinite period! This woman, who was doubtless most efficient at all other times, seemed positively disturbed when, in reply to her enquiry after my luggage, I told her that it would be brought along that evening by an officer from the Oberjoch customs post.

Insofar as I could tell with any certainty, given the structural changes that had been made in the Engelwirt, the room allocated to me was approximately where our living room had once been, the room which was furnished with all the pieces my parents had bought in 1936 when, after two or three years of continuous upturn in the country's fortunes, it seemed assured that my father, who at the calamitous close of the Weimar era had enlisted in the so-called army of the One Hundred Thousand and was now about to be promoted to quartermaster, could not only look forward to a secure future in the new Reich but could even be said to have attained a certain social position. For my parents, both of whom came from provincial backwaters, my mother from W. and my father from the Bavarian Forest, the acquisition of living room furniture befitting their station, which, as the unwritten rule required, had to conform in every detail with the tastes of the average couple representative of the emerging classless society, probably marked the moment when, in the wake of their in some respects rather difficult early lives, it must have seemed to them as if there were, after all, something like a higher justice. This living room, then, boasted a ponderously ornate armoire, in which were kept the tablecloths, napkins, silver cutlery, Christmas decorations and, behind the glass doors of the upper half, the bone china tea service which, as far as I can remember, was never brought out on a single occasion; a sideboard on which an earthenware punchbowl glazed in peculiar hues and two so-called lead crystal flower vases were placed symmetrically on crocheted doilies; the draw-leaf dining table with a set of six chairs; a sofa with an assortment of embroidered cushions; on the wall behind it two small Alpine landscapes in black varnished frames, the one hung a little higher than the other; a smokers' table with gaudily coloured ceramic cigar and cigarette containers and matching candlestick, an ashtray made of horn and brass, and an electric smoke absorber in the shape of an owl. In addition, apart from the drapes and net curtains, ceiling lights and standard lamp, there was a flower *étagère* made of bamboo cane, on the various levels of which an Araucaria, an asparagus fern, a Christmas cactus and a passion flower led their strictly regulated plant lives. It should also be mentioned that on the top of the armoire stood the living room clock which counted out the hours with its cold and loveless chimes, and that in the upper half of the armoire, next to the bone china tea service, was a row of clothbound dramatic works by Shakespeare, Schiller, Hebbel and Sudermann. These were inexpensive editions published by the Volksbühnenverband, which my father, who would probably never have taken it into his head to go to the theatre, and less still to read a play, had bought one day, in a passing moment of aspiration to higher ideals, from a travelling salesman. The guest room through the window of which I now looked down into the street was a world away from all of that; I myself, though, was no more than a breath away, and if the living room clock had started chiming in my sleep, I would not have been in the least surprised.

Like most of the houses in W., the Engelwirt was separated lengthwise into two sections by a broad passageway on both floors. On the ground floor, the function room was on one side, on the other the public bar, the kitchen, the ice store, and the *pissoir*. On the upper floor, the one-legged landlord Sallaba, who had turned up in W. after the war to take over the tenancy together with his beautiful wife, who regarded the village always as an odious place, had set up his household. Sallaba possessed a large number of stylish suits and ties with tie-pins; but it was not so much his wardrobe, which was indeed exceptional for W., as his one-leggedness and the astonishing speed and virtuosity with which he moved about on his crutches that gave him the air of a man of the world in my eyes. Sallaba was said to be a Rhinelander, a term which remained a mystery to me for a long time and which I supposed to be a character trait. Apart from the Sallabas and ourselves, the erstwhile landlady of the Engelwirt, Rosina Zobel, also lived on the first floor; she had given up running the inn several years ago and ever since had spent the entire day in her partially darkened parlour. She either sat in her wing chair, or walked back and forth, or lay on the sofa. No one knew whether it was red wine that had made her melancholy or whether it was because of her melancholy that she had turned to red wine. She was never seen doing any work; she did not shop, or cook, nor was she to be seen laundering clothes or tidying the room. Only once did I see her in the garden with a knife in her hand and a bunch of chives, looking up into the pear tree which had recently come into leaf. The door to the Engelwirt landlady's room was usually left slightly ajar, and I frequently went in to her and would spend hours looking at the collection of postcards she kept in three large folio volumes. The landlady, wine glass in hand, sometimes sat next to me at the table as I browsed, but only ever spoke to tell me the name of the town I happened to be pointing to. As the minutes passed by this resulted in a long topographical litany of place names such as Chur, Bregenz, Innsbruck, Altaussee, Hallstatt, Salzburg, Vienna, Pilsen, Marienbad, Bad Kissingen, Würzburg, Bad Homburg and Frankfurt am Main. There were also numerous Italian cards from Merano, Bolzano, Riva, Verona, Milan, Ferrara, Rome and Naples. One of these postcards, showing the smoking peak of Vesuvius, somehow or other got into an album belonging to my parents, and so has come into my

possession. The third volume contained pictures from overseas, particularly from the Far East, from Dutch South East Asia, and from China and Japan. This collection of postcards, which ran to several hundred in all, had been put together by Rosina Zobel's husband, old Engelwirt, who before marrying Rosina had travelled far and wide, spending the greater part of a considerable inheritance, and who had now been bedridden for a number of years. People said that he lay in the room adjoining Rosina's and had a large wound in his hip which would not heal. They said that as a youngster he had tried to hide a cigar, which he had been secretly smoking, from his father, and had put it in his trouser pocket. The burn he had sustained had soon mended, but later, when he was nearly fifty, it opened up again and now refused to close at all, indeed it became larger every year, and he might well, so they said, end up dying of gangrene. I considered this statement, which I could not understand, to be some sort of judgement, and I envisioned the Engelwirt's martyrdom in all the colours of hellfire. I never saw him in person, though, and, as far as I can remember, the landlady, who in any case spoke very little, never once mentioned him. On a couple of occasions, however, I thought I heard him wheezing in the other room. Later on, as time went by, it seemed to me less and less likely that the Engelwirt landlord had existed at all, and I wondered if I had not simply imagined him. However, further enquiries in W. left no room for doubt in the matter. It also transpired that the children of the Engelwirt couple, Johannes and Magdalena, who were not much older than I, had been brought up elsewhere by an aunt, as the Engelwirt landlady had started drinking heavily after the birth of Magdalena and had no longer been capable of looking after the children. Towards me, perhaps because I was otherwise not in her charge, the landlady showed endless patience. Not infrequently I sat in bed with her, she at the head and I at the foot, and recited everything to her that I knew by heart, including of course the Lord's Prayer, the Angelus and other orisons which had not passed her lips for a very long time. I can still see her as she listened to me, head inclined against the bedstead, eyes closed, the glass and bottle of Kalterer wine on the marble top of the table beside her, expressions of pain and relief crossing her face in turn. It was also from her that I learned how to tie a bow; and whenever I left the room she laid her hand upon me. To this day I can sometimes feel her thumb against my forehead.

Across the street from the Engelwirt inn was the Seelos house, where the Ambrose family lived. My mother was often there because she was very close to the Ambrose children who, some ten years younger than she, had frequently been looked after by her when they were growing up. The Ambroses had come to W. during the last century from Imst in the Tyrol, and whenever there was fault to be found with them, they were still referred to as the Tyroleans. Otherwise, though they were named after the house that they had taken over, and were generally not called the Ambroses, but Seelos Maria, Seelos Lena, Seelos Benedikt, Seelos Lukas and Seelos Regina. Seelos Maria was a large, slow-moving woman who had worn black since the death, several years before, of her husband Baptist, and spent her days making coffee in the Turkish fashion, perhaps in memory of Baptist, who had been a master builder and had been employed in that capacity in Constantinople for eighteen months before the First World War, from where, no doubt, he brought with him the true art of coffee-making. Nearly all the larger buildings in W. and the surrounding area, the school, the railway station in Haslach and the turbine powerhouse, which supplied the entire district with electricity, had been designed on the drawing board of Ambrose and constructed under his supervision. He had died of a stroke, much too young as they always used to say, on May Day, 1933. He was found in his workplace, collapsed over the blueprint apparatus, a pencil behind his ear and a pair of compasses still in his hand. The Seelos family lived on what Baptist had left, and on the income from the fields and the two houses that he had acquired during his lifetime. Baptist's workplace was later rented out, curiously enough to a Turk of about twenty-five named Ekrem, who, from God knows where, had arrived in W. after the "Umsturz", as the end of the War was referred to, and who spent his time making large quantities of Turkish delight in the kitchen, which he then sold at fairs. Perhaps it was Ekrem who taught Seelos Maria how to brew mocha, and who found ways of procuring the precious black beans of which Maria always had a supply, even in the hardest of times. One day Seelos Lena was delivered of a child of

Ekrem's, but fortunately, as I heard people say, it lived for only a week. I well remember the tiny white infant's coffin on the heavy black hearse being drawn to the cemetery by our neighbour's pair of black horses, and the rainwater running down off the pile of clay into the small grave during the interment. Soon afterwards, if not even before, Ekrem disappeared from W., to Munich as rumour had it, where he was said to have set up as a tropical fruit merchant, and Lena emigrated to California, where she married a telephone engineer, with whom she was killed in a car accident.

The Seelos family also included the three unmarried sisters of Baptist, the Aunts Babett, Bina and Mathild, who lived in the house next door, and bachelor Uncle Peter, who had been a wheelwright with his workshop at the back of the Seelos house. In the years after the war, when he would have been about sixty, he took to walking around the village and would watch people at their work. Only rarely did he pick up a hoe or a fork himself and poke about with it in the yard or the garden. I never knew Peter to be any different, for it was already many a year since, little by little, he had begun to lose his mind. At first he neglected his business as a wheelwright, taking on commissions but only half finishing them, and then he turned to producing complicated pseudo-architectural plans, such as one for a water house built over the river Ach, or another for a forest pulpit, a sort of spiral stairs-cum-platform, which was to have encircled one of the tallest pines in the parish woods, and from the top of which the parish priest was to have made a speech to his trees on a certain day every year. Most of these plans, unfortunately lost, of which Peter drew up page after page, he never seriously tackled. The only one actually realised was what he called the Salettl, which was built into the roof of the Seelos house, a wooden platform being erected about a metre below the ridge, and raised upon this, once the tiles were removed, a timber framework for a glass observatory that reached through and above the ridge. From this vantage-point one could see over the rooftops of the village far out into the high moors and the fields and right across to the dark shadowy mountains rising up from the valley. The completion of the Salettl took some time, and after he had held a solitary topping-out ceremony all on his own, Peter did not come down from his observation post for weeks. It was said that he spent a large part of the first years of the war up there, sleeping by day and watching the stars by night, drawing the constellations on large deep blue sheets of card, or alternatively perforating them by means of bradawls of varying sizes so that, when he attached the sheets to the wooden frames of his glass house, he could actually enjoy the illusion, as in a planetarium, that the star-lit heavens were vaulted above his head. Towards the end of the war, when Seelos Benedikt, who had always been a timorous child, was sent to a school for non-commissioned officers at Rastatt,

Peter's condition deteriorated noticeably. At times
he would wander about the
village with a cape cut from
his charts of the night sky,
talking of how one could
see the stars by day both
from the bottom of a well
and from the peaks of the
highest mountains, which
was probably the consola-
tion he offered himself for
the circumstance that now,
every evening at the onset

of darkness which formerly he had always welcomed, he was beset with so great a fear that he had to cover his ears with his hands or flail about wildly. It was because of this condition that a sort of closet was built for him on the half-landing where his bed was installed, and which he soon went into of his own accord in the late afternoons. From that time onwards, the Salettl was no longer used. Not till the sawmill burned down did anyone think of the lookout again. Then we all climbed up to the Salettl, with the whole of the Seelos family and most of their neighbours, to watch the enormous fire blazing into the sky and lighting from below the pall of smoke drifting a long way out. But Uncle Peter was not with us. That same year when the sawmill burned down, he was admitted to the hospital in Pfronten, for suddenly no one, not even Regina, the most beautiful of the Seelos children and the one whom he liked the best, could get him to eat a thing. Peter would not stay in the hospital, though, but was up and away the very first night, leaving a note which read: *My dear Doctor! I have gone to the Tyrol. Yours most sincerely, Peter Ambrose.* The ensuing search failed to find him, and to this day he has not been heard of again.

For the first week of my sojourn in W. I did not leave the Engelwirt inn. Troubled by dreams at night and getting no peace till the first light of dawn, I slept through the entire morning. I spent the afternoons sitting in the empty bar room, turning over my recollections and writing up my notes, and in the evenings when the regulars came in, whom I recognised, almost to a man, from my schooldays and who all appeared to have grown older at a stroke, I listened to their talk while pretending to read the newspaper, never tiring of it and ordering one glass of Kalterer after the other. Hunched over the long table they sat, most as in the old days with their hats on their heads, under an enormous picture of wood-cutters at work. This painting, which had hung in the same place in the old Engelwirt inn, had by now become so black-ened that it was scarcely possible to make out what it actually portrayed. Not till one had looked at it for some time did the phantom shapes of the woodcutters become apparent. They were in the process of stripping and clamping the timber, and were painted in the powerful, energetic postures characteristic of images that glorify work and warfare. The artist Hengge, by whom, without any doubt, this picture was done, had produced many such woodcutter scenes in his time. His fame reached its peak in the 1930s, when he was known as far afield as Munich. His murals, always in dark shades of brown, were to be seen on the walls of buildings all around W. and the surrounding area, and were always of his favoured motifs of woodcutters, deer poachers and rebellious peasants carry-ing the Bundschuh-banner unless a particular theme had been requested of him. On the Seefelders house, for example, where my grandfather lived and where I was born, a motor race was depicted, because it had seemed to old Seefelder, a blacksmith by trade, to go with the machine workshop he had set up a couple of years before the war, and appropriate

also to the new age which was then dawning in W., and the transformer station on the edge of the village was adorned with an allegorical representation of the taming of the power of water. For me there was something most unsettling about

all of these Hengge pictures. One especially, on the Raiffeisen Bank, showing a tall reaper woman, sickle in hand, standing

in front of a field at harvest time, always looked to me like a fearful battle scene, and frightened me so that whenever I passed, I had to avert my eyes. Hengge the painter was perfectly capable of extending his repertoire. But whenever he was able to follow his own artistic inclination, he would paint only pictures of woodcutters. Even after the war, when for a variety of reasons his monumental works were no longer much in demand, he continued in the same vein. In the end, his house was said to have been so crammed with pictures of woodcutters that there was scarcely room for Hengge himself, and death, so the obituary said, caught him in the midst of a work showing a woodcutter on a sledge hurtling down into the valley below. On reflection, it had occurred to me that those Hengge paintings, apart from the frescoes in the parish church, were pretty much the only pictures I had seen until I was seven or eight years old, and I now have the feeling that these woodcutters and the crucifixions and the large canvas of the Battle of the Lechfeld, where Prince Bishop Ulrich, astride his grey charger, rides over one of the Huns lying prostrate on the ground – and here again all the horses have this crazed look in their eyes – made a devastating impression on me. For that reason, when I had reached a certain point in my notes, I left my post in the Engelwirt bar to see the Hengge murals once more, or those that were still there. I cannot say that their effect on me on re-acquaintance was any less devastating, rather the contrary. At all events I found that as I went from one of his works to another I was drawn onward, and I walked through the fields and towards the outlying hamlets

on the surrounding mountainsides and hills. I made my way up to Bichl and walked on to the Adelharz, to Enthalb der Ach, to Bärenwinkel and Jungholz, into the Vordere and the Hintere Reutte, out to Haslach and Oy, into the Schrey and from there on to Elleg, all of them paths that

I had walked in my childhood at my grandfather's side and which had meant so much to me in my memory, but, as I came to realise, meant nothing to me now. From every one of these excursions I returned dispirited to the Engelwirt and to the writing of my notes, which had afforded me a degree of comfort of late, even as the example of Hengge the artist, and the questionable nature of painting as an enterprise in general, remained before me as a warning.

I had learned that the only member of the Seelos family still living in W. was Lukas. The Seelos house had been sold, and Lukas lodged in the smaller house next door, where once Babett, Bina and Mathild had dwelt. I had been in W. for about ten days before I finally decided to go over and call on Lukas. He had seen me coming out of the Engelwirt several times, he told me straight away, but although I had somehow seemed familiar, he had not quite been able to place me, perhaps because I reminded him not so much of the child I once was as of my grandfather who had the same gait and, whenever he stepped out of the house, would pause for a moment to peer up into the sky to see what the weather was doing, just as I always did. I felt my visit pleased Lukas, for after working as a tin-roofer until his fiftieth year he had been forced into retirement by the arthritis that was gradually crippling him, and now spent his days sitting at home on the sofa, while his wife continued to run the little stationer's shop belonging to old Specht. He would never have believed, he observed, how long the days, and time, and life itself could be when one had been shunted aside. Moreover, he was troubled by the fact that, apart from Regina, who was married to an industrialist in northern Germany, he was the last of the Ambrose clan. He told me the story of how Uncle Peter disappeared in the Tyrol, and of the death of his mother soon afterwards, who during the last weeks of her life had lost so much of her considerable weight that nobody had recognised her any more; and he expatiated at length on the strange circumstance that Aunts Babett and Bina, who had done everything together since they were children, had died on the same day, one of heart failure and the other of grief. No one had ever been able to find out much, he said, about the car accident in America in which Lena and her husband were killed. It seemed that the two of them simply left the road in their Oldsmobile, which as he knew from a photo had whitewall tyres, and plunged into the depths. Mathild had lasted a long time, until she was well over eighty, perhaps because she had the most alert mind of any of them. She had died a quiet death in her own bed in the middle of the night. His wife, Lukas said, had found her the next day, lying just as she always did when she retired in the evening. But Benedikt, unwilling to go further into the subject, had been consumed by ill fortune and now, he added, it was his own turn. Having brought to an end his chronicle of the Ambrose family with this remark, not without satisfaction as it seemed to me, Lukas wanted to know what had brought me back to W. after so many years, and in November of all times. To my surprise, he understood my rather complicated and sometimes contradictory explanations right away. He particularly agreed when I said that over the years I had puzzled out a good deal in my own mind, but in spite of that, far from becoming clearer, things now appeared to me more incomprehensible than ever. The more images I gathered from the past, I said, the more unlikely it seemed to me that the past had actually happened in this or that way, for nothing about it could be called normal: most of it was absurd, and if not absurd, then appalling. To which Lukas replied that now, laid up as he was on his sofa for much of the day or at best performing pointless little tasks about the house, it was quite unthinkable that he had once been a good goalkeeper and that he, who was ever more frequently assailed by dark moods, had in his time played the clown round the village – had indeed held for years, as I perhaps remembered, the honorary office of carnival jester since a successor was not to be found who could hold a candle to him. As he recalled that glorious time, Lukas's gouty hands began to move more freely, demonstrating how one grasped the great carnival shears, which he said required exceptional strength and poise, and how he had stuck his fool's staff up the women's skirts at the very moment when they least expected it. Just as they imagined themselves safe, behind locked doors on the top floor, and were leaning out of the windows to watch as the carnival floats passed by, he had climbed up at the back through the hay loft, or up an espalier, and given them the fright they were hoping for all along, though they would never admit as much. Often he had ducked into the kitchen and filched the freshly baked doughnuts in order to distribute them in the street to the applause of the women until, seeing the empty plates, they realised it was their own doughnuts that had been handed out.

From such carnival exploits, our talk turned to Specht the printer, whose stationer's shop Lukas's wife was now running. For Specht, as Lukas said, had invariably still had his Christmas tree in his shop window when carnival week came round; indeed, that tree, which he had put up during the last week of Advent and which was now quite bare of needles, remained in the window not only until carnival but frequently until Easter, and on one occasion Specht even had to be reminded to remove the tree from the window in time at least for the Corpus Christi procession. Specht, who since the 1920s had written, edited, set and printed the fortnightly four-page newspaper *Der Landbote*, was an extremely introverted fellow, as is not infrequently the case

with printers. Moreover, the constant handling of lead type had made him ever smaller and greyer. I had a clear memory of Specht, from whom I had bought my first slate pencils and later the pens and the exercise books made of pulp paper on which the nibs constantly stuck when one was writing. Year in, year out he wore a grey calico coat which almost reached down to the floor, and round steel spectacles, and, whenever you entered the shop beneath the jingling bell, he would emerge from the printroom at the back with an oil rag in his hand. In the evenings, though, he could be seen sitting in the lamplight at the kitchen table, writing the articles and reports which were to be included in *Der Landbote*. Lukas claimed that much of what Specht wrote week after week for *Der Landbote* was rejected by him in his capacity as editor as not being up to the standards of the paper. Later on, when we had run out of Kalterer wine, Lukas took me around the house, showed me where Babett's and Bina's café, the Alpenrose, had been, where Dr Rambousek had his surgery, and where the bedrooms and the living room of the three sisters once were. As I was leaving, Lukas clutched my hand in the birdlike grasp of his gouty fingers for a long time, and I said that I would be glad to come over to see him more often so that we might talk further about the past, if he did not mind. Yes, said Lukas, there was something strange about remembering. When he lay on the sofa and thought back, it all became blurred as if he was out in a fog.

That same evening, over a second bottle of Kalterer in the Engelwirt, I was able to assemble some of my recollections of the Alpenrose. Whether it was Babett and Bina who had the idea of opening the café, or whether Baptist thought that it would support his unmarried sisters, was a part of the story that nobody could recall any more. At all events, there had been a Café Alpenrose, and it had continued until the deaths of Babett and Bina, although nobody had ever set foot in it. In summer, a small green metal table and three green folding chairs stood in the front garden under a pollarded lime tree which afforded a fine broad canopy of leaves. The door of the house was always open, and every couple of minutes Bina would appear in order to look out for the guests who would, surely, be arriving sometime. There is no way of telling what kept visitors away. Probably it was not simply because strangers, as summer guests were referred to in those days, hardly ever came to stay in W., but rather because the coffee house was run by Babett and Bina as a sort of spinsters' parlour which had nothing to offer the men of the village. I do not know, nor did Lukas know, what sort of figure the two sisters had made at the beginning of their business venture. The only thing that could be said with any certainty was that whatever Babett and Bina had been at one time, or had wanted to be, was eventually destroyed by the years of continuous disappointment and perennially revived hope. The impairment to their lives which that destruction and their unending dependency on each other entailed ultimately led to their being regarded as no more than a pair of dotty old maids. Of course it did not help that Bina, smoothing down her apron with her hands, spent the hours running around the house and the front garden, while Babett sat in the kitchen all day long folding tea towels, only to unfold and refold them again. It was with the greatest effort that the two of them managed to keep their small household in order, and what they would have done if one day a guest had actually crossed the threshold is quite inconceivable. Even when making a pot of soup they were more of a hindrance than a help to each other, and the weekly creation of a cake for Sunday, Lukas told me, was always a major operation that took them the whole of Saturday. Nonetheless, whenever the end of the week was approaching, Babett would prevail upon Bina, as much as Bina prevailed upon Babett, that a cake should be baked once again, alternately either an apple cake or a so-called *Guglhupf.* Once the task was accomplished, the cake would be carried with some ceremony into the front room and there, virginal and freshly dusted with icing sugar, as it was, placed under a glass dome on the sideboard, next to the apple cake, or else the *Guglhupf,* that had been baked the previous Saturday, so that any guest who had happened by on the Saturday afternoon would have had a choice of two cakes – a stale apple cake and a fresh *Guglhupf* or a stale *Guglhupf* and a fresh apple cake. On the Sunday afternoon that choice ceased to be available, for it was always on Sunday afternoons that Babett and Bina consumed either the stale apple cake or the stale *Guglhupf* with their Sunday afternoon coffee, Babett eating the cake with a cake fork while Bina would be dunking hers, a habit which Babett deplored and which she had never been able to correct in her sister. After consuming the stale cake the two of them would sit for an hour or two, sated and silent, in the gloom of their parlour. On the wall over the sideboard hung a picture of two lovers in the act of committing suicide. It was a winter night and the moon had emerged from behind the clouds to witness this final moment. The pair, out on a narrow landing stage, were about to take their last decisive step. Together, the foot of the girl and that of the man were suspended over the dark waters, and one could sense with relief how both were now in the grip of gravity. I remember that the girl had a thin, viridescent veil draped over her head, while the man's coat was taut against the wind. Below this picture stood the cake intended for the coming week; the clock on the wall ticked, and whenever it was about to strike it gave a long-drawn-out wheeze, as if it could not bring itself to announce the loss of another quarter of an hour. In summer, the light of late afternoon entered through the curtains, in winter the falling dusk, and on the table in the centre, biding its time, stood the enormous aspidistra which the long years had left untouched and around which, in some mysterious manner, everything at the Alpenrose seemed to revolve.

My grandfather went across to the Alpenrose once a week to call upon Mathild. The two of them usually played several games of cards together and conversed at some length, as there was always plenty to talk about. They would sit in the front parlour, for Mathild did not allow anyone, not even Grandfather, up to her room; Babett and Bina, who respected Mathild as a higher authority, had become accustomed to remain in the kitchen during these visits. I often accompanied my grandfather to the Alpenrose, just as I accompanied him almost everywhere, and there I sat with a diluted raspberry syrup as the cards were shuffled, cut, dealt, played, placed to one side, counted and shuffled again. My grandfather was in the habit of wearing his hat while playing cards, and not until the last game was finished and Mathild had gone out into the kitchen to brew the coffee did he take off the hat and then wipe his forehead with his handkerchief. Of the matters discussed over coffee, there were few I had any notion of, and for that reason, once they started talking together, I generally went out into the front garden, sat on one of the chairs by the green metal table and looked at the old atlas which Mathild put out for me every time. In this atlas there was a page on which the longest rivers and the highest elevations on the surface of the

Vertigo

Earth were arranged by length or height, and there were wonderfully coloured maps, even of the most distant, scarcely discovered continents, with legends in tiny lettering which, perhaps because I could decipher them only in part just like the early cartographers were able to picture only parts of the world, appeared to me to hold in them all conceivable mysteries. During the colder months of the year I would sit with the atlas on my knees on the top landing, where the light came in through the staircase window and an oleograph hung on the wall showing a wild boar making a gigantic leap out of the gloom of the forest to scatter hunters at their breakfast in a clearing. The scene, in which, quite apart from the boar and the frightened green-coated hunters, the plates and sausages flying through the air were depicted with great attention to detail, was inscribed *Im Ardennerwald*, and this caption, innocent in itself, evoked for me something far more dangerous, unknown and profound than the picture by itself could ever have conjured up. The secret contained in the word "Ardennerwald" was deepened by the fact that Mathild had expressly forbidden me to open any of the doors on the top floor. Above all, I was not to climb up into the attic which, as Mathild had given me to understand in her peculiarly persuasive manner, was the dwelling of someone she referred to as the grey *chasseur*, about whom she would not tell me any more. So on the landing to the first floor I was, as it were, on the borderline of what was permissible, at the point where the lure of temptation could be most keenly sensed. For that reason I always felt as though I had been rescued when my grandfather at last emerged from the coffee room, put his hat on his head, and shook hands with Mathild in farewell.

When I next saw Lukas, we went up to the attic which I must have mentioned in our conversations. Lukas was of the opinion that not much could have changed up there since those days. He had never cleared out the attic when he took over the house after his aunts died, he said, for this, even then, would have been beyond his powers, given that the whole space was cluttered to the rafters with all manner of implements and miscellaneous lumber and one thing piled on top of another. The attic was indeed a daunting sight. Boxes and baskets were stacked high, sacks, leather gear, doorbells, ropes, mousetraps, beehive frames and cases for all kinds of instruments were hanging from the beams. In a corner a bass tuba still glinted from beneath the layer of dust covering it, and next to it, on an eiderdown that had once been red, lay an enormous, long abandoned wasps' nest, both of them – the brass tuba and the fragile grey paper shell – tokens of the slow disintegration of all material forms in the complete silence of this attic. And yet that silence was not to be trusted. Out of trunks, chests, and wardrobes, some with their lids, drawers and doors half open, all conceivable kinds of utensils and garments were bursting forth. It was easy to imagine that this entire assemblage of the most diverse objects had been moving, in some sort of secret evolution, until the moment we entered, and that it was only because of our presence that these things now held their breath as if nothing had happened. On a shelf that immediately attracted my attention was Mathild's library, comprising almost a hundred volumes, which have since come into my possession and are proving ever more important to me. Besides various literary works from the last century, accounts of expeditions to the polar regions, textbooks on geometry and structural engineering, and a Turkish dictionary complete with a manual for the writing of letters, which had probably once belonged to Baptist, there were numerous religious works of a speculative character, and prayer-books dating back two or three hundred years, with illustrations, some of them perfectly gruesome, showing the torments and travails that await us all. In among the devotional works, to my amazement, there were several treatises by Bakunin, Fourier, Bebel, Eisner, and Landauer, and an autobiographical novel by the socialist Lily von Braun. When I enquired

OFFICIUM
Für die abgestorbene Seelen in dem
Fegfeur.

about the origins of the books, Lukas was able to tell me
only that Mathild had always been a great reader, and
because of this, as I might perhaps remember, was thought
of by the villagers as peculiar, if not deranged. Just before
the First World War she had entered the convent of the
Englische Fräulein in Regensburg, but had left there, for
reasons which were never made clear to Lukas, before the

end of the war, and subsequently had spent several months in Munich during the time of the ill-fated Red Republic, returning home to W. in a seriously disturbed and almost speechless state. He himself, Lukas said, had of course not been born by then, but he well remembered his mother making a remark about how Mathild had been quite unhinged when she came back to W. from the convent and from Communist Munich. Occasionally, when his mother was in a bad mood, she even called Mathild a bigoted Bolshevik. Mathild for her part, however, once she had regained something of her equilibrium, did not allow herself to be put out in the slightest by such remarks. To the contrary, said Lukas, she evidently came to feel quite comfortable in her detachment, and indeed the way in which, year after year, she went about among the villagers whom she despised, forever dressed in a black frock or a black coat, and always in a hat and never, even in the finest weather, without an umbrella, had, as I might remember from my own childhood days, something blissful about it.

As I continued to look around in the attic, picking up this and that, a hairless china doll, a goldfinch cage, a target rifle, or an old calf-hide knapsack, and discussing the possible provenance and history of these items with Lukas, I became aware of something like an apparition, a uniformed figure, which now could be seen more clearly, now more faintly behind the blade of light that slanted through the attic window. On closer inspection it revealed itself as an old tailor's dummy, dressed in pike-grey breeches and a pike-grey jacket, the collar, cuffs and edgings of which must once have been grass green, and the buttons a golden yellow. On its wooden headpiece the dummy was wearing a hat, also pike-grey, with a bunch of cockerel's tail feathers in it. Perhaps because it had been concealed behind the shaft of light that cut through the darkness of the attic and in which swirled the glinting particles of matter dissolving into weightlessness, the grey figure instantly made a most uncanny impression on me, an impression which was only intensified by the smell of camphor exuding from it. But when I stepped closer, not entirely trusting my eyes, and touched one of the uniform sleeves that hung down empty, to my utter horror it crumbled into dust. From what I have been able to discover since, that uniform, trimmed in the colours pike-grey and green, almost certainly belonged to one of the Austrian *chasseurs* who fought against the French as irregulars around 1800, a conjecture that gained in plausibility when Lukas told me a story which also went back to Mathild. It seems that one of the more distant Seelos forebears led a contingent of one thousand men levied in the Tyrol across the Brenner

Pass, down the Adige, past Lake Garda and onto the upper Italian plains, and there, with all his troops, was killed in the terrible Battle of Marengo. The significance for me of this tale of a Tyrolean *chasseur* who had fallen at Marengo lay not least in the realisation that, in the attic of the Café Alpenrose, which, on my childhood visits, I had been forbidden to go up into on account of it being the haunt of the grey *chasseur*, there had truly been such a *chasseur*, even if he did not correspond in every respect to the picture I had formed of him while sitting on the landing. What I had fantasised at the time, and what later often appeared to me in my dreams, was a tall stranger with a high round cap of astrakhan fur set low on his forehead, dressed in a brown greatcoat fastened with broad straps reminiscent of a horse's harness. Lying in his lap he had a short curved sabre with a sheath that gleamed faintly. His feet were encased in spurred jackboots. One foot was on an overturned wine bottle, the other he rested up-angled on the floor, the heel and spur rammed into the wood. Time and again I dreamed, and occasionally still do, that this stranger reaches out his hand to me and I, in the teeth of my fear, venture ever closer to him, so close that, at last, I can touch him. And every time, I then see before me the fingers of my right hand, dusty and even blackened from that one touch, like the token of some great woe that nothing in the world will ever put right.

Until the end of the 1940s Dr Rudolf Rambousek had his practice in the Alpenrose, in the ground floor room opposite the coffee and wine bar. Dr Rambousek had come to W. not long after the end of the war, from a Moravian town, I believe from Nikolsburg, with his pallid wife and his two adolescent daughters Felicia and Amalia, and for him, and no less for his women, this must have been banishment to the ends of the earth. It was no surprise that this short, corpulent man, who was always dressed like a man about town, was unable to gain a foothold in W. His melancholy and foreign-seeming features, perhaps best described as Levantine, the way his lids were always lowered over his large, dark eyes, and his entire somehow distant demeanour, left little doubt that he was one of those who are born to lead inconsolable lives. To my knowledge Dr Rambousek did not befriend a single person during the years he spent in W. He was said to be withdrawn, and it is true that I cannot remember ever having seen him in the street, although he did not live in the Alpenrose but in the teacher's house and must therefore occasionally have been on his way either from the teacher's house to the Alpenrose or from the Alpenrose to the teacher's house. It was not least by virtue of his positively conspicuous absence that he was altogether different from Dr Piazolo, who must already have been approaching seventy and could be seen at every hour of the day and night riding his 750 Zündapp around the village or up and downhill to the outlying hamlets. In winter and summer alike Dr Piazolo, who in emergencies was willing to take on veterinary work without thinking twice about it and who had evidently resolved to die in the saddle, wore an old aviator's cap with earflaps, enormous motorcycling goggles, a leather outfit and leather gaiters. It is also worth mentioning that Dr Piazolo had a double or shadow rider in the priest Father Wurmser, who was also no longer one of the youngest, and who for a good while had been making his visits to the dying on his motorcycle, carrying all that was necessary to perform the last rites, the consecrated oil, holy water, salt, a small silver crucifix and the holy sacrament, with him in an old rucksack which was exactly the same as the one belonging to Dr Piazolo. On one occasion the two of them, the priest and Dr Piazolo, mistook each other's rucksacks when they were sitting side by side at the Adlerwirt, and Dr Piazolo drove off to his next patient equipped for the last rites while Father Wurmser brought the doctor's instruments to the next member of his congregation who was about to expire. The similarity not only of the rucksacks belonging to Father Wurmser and Dr Piazolo but also of their general appearance was such that if you saw a dark motorcyclist somewhere in the village or on the roads outside the village, it would have been impossible to say whether it was the doctor or the parson, had it not been for the doctor's habit, while riding his motorcycle, of letting his feet, on which he wore hobnailed boots, drag through the gravel or snow on the road rather than placing them on the foot-rests, which meant that, at least when seen from the front or behind, he cut a different figure from the parson. It is easy to imagine how difficult it must have been for Dr Rambousek to take on his well-established competitors, and to see why he preferred, in contrast to these two as it were omnipresent emissaries, the priest and the physician, not to leave the house at all. Yet, it would be wrong to suggest that Dr Rambousek did not enjoy the esteem of those who went to him. I more than once heard my mother extolling the medical skills of Dr Rambousek in the highest possible terms, particularly when talking to Valerie Schwarz, the milliner, who came not from Moravia like Dr Rambousek but from Bohemia, and who, despite her shortness, had a bosom of a size that I have only seen on one occasion since, on the tobacconist in Fellini's film *Amarcord*. But while my mother and Valerie could not praise Dr Rambousek highly enough, the other villagers would never have dreamed of going to his surgery. If something was the matter, you simply sent for Dr Piazolo, and that was why Dr Rambousek spent most of his time, day after day, month after month and year after year, sitting alone in his surgery in the Alpenrose. At any rate, when I went across to Mathild with my grandfather I always saw him through the half-open door in the sparsely furnished room, sitting in his swivel chair and writing or reading or simply staring out of the window. Once or twice I quietly stepped onto the threshold and waited for him to look across at me or ask me to come closer, but either he never noticed my presence or he did not feel able to address the strange child. One exceptionally hot day in the midsummer of 1949, when Grandfather and Mathild were conversing in the front room, I sat for a long time on the topmost step of the stairs that led up to the attic, listening to the creaking of the roof timbers and the few other noises, such as the rising and falling screech of a circular saw or the solitary crowing of a cockerel, that came into the house from outside. Before my grandfather's visiting time was ended, I went down into the hall passageway, having determined to ask Dr Rambousek if he was not perhaps capable of healing the old Engelwirt landlord's open sore that grew larger by the day, and to my bewilderment, found the door to the surgery closed. Cautiously, I pressed down the handle. Inside, everything was bathed in the deep green summer light that filtered through the leaves of the lime tree outside the window. The silence that surrounded me seemed boundless. As was his wont, Dr Rambousek was sitting on his swivel chair, except that his body was leaning forwards onto the desk. The left shirt sleeve was rolled halfway up, and in the crook of the elbow, turned sideways at an odd angle, rested the doctor's head, seeming somehow outsize, with its dark, slightly protruding but still beautiful eyes staring fixedly into the void. I left the surgery on tiptoe and climbed back up to my station right at the top of the attic stairs, where I waited until I heard my grandfather coming out of the parlour with Mathild. Not a word about Dr Rambousek did I breathe to my grandfather, both out of fear and because I myself could scarcely believe what I had seen. On the way home we had to pick up the fob watch he had left to be repaired at Ebentheuer's the watchmaker. The doorbell clanged, and there we were, standing in the small shop in which a host of long-case clocks, wall-mounted regulators, kitchen and living room clocks, alarm clocks, pocket and wrist watches were all ticking at once, just as if one clock on its own could not destroy enough time. While Grandfather talked to Ebentheuer, who, as always, had his watchmaker's glass jammed into his left eye, about what had been wrong with his fob watch, I looked across the shop counter into the half-lit living room where the youngest of the Ebentheuer children, who was called Eustach and had water on the brain, was sitting on a high chair, rocking gently back and forth. As for Dr Rambousek, he was found the same evening lifeless and cold in the surgery of the Alpenrose by his wife, who shortly afterwards moved away from W. together with her two daughters. Later I once overheard Valerie Schwarz whisper to my mother that Dr Rambousek had been a morphine addict or morphinist, as she put it, and that hence his skin was often tainted yellow. Because of this to me incomprehensible remark, I believed for a long time that people born in Moravia were called morphinists and that they came from a country quite as far away as Mongolia or China.

During the years when we lived above the Engelwirt, I would unfailingly, in the early evenings, be seized by the desire to go down to the taproom to help Romana wipe the tables and benches, sweep the floor or dry the glasses. It was not, of course, these chores but Romana herself who drew me and in whose company I conspired to spend as much time as I possibly could. Romana was the elder of two daughters of a family of small-holders who, in the hamlet of Bärenwinkel, rented a few patches of land and a crooked, timber-framed house which, toysized in comparison with the other farmsteads, stood all by itself on a hillock and always reminded me of the story of Noah, especially as in and around it there appeared to be two of every kind – apart from the parents and the two sisters, Romana and Lisabeth, there was a cow and a bull, two goats, two pigs, two geese, and so on. There were larger numbers only of cats and hens, and they sat or scratched about way into the surrounding fields. There were also a sizeable flock of white doves which, when they were not clambering back and forth over the ridge, soared above and around the little house which, with its shingled and much-mended hipped roof, unusual for the area, looked for all the world like the biblical Ark stranded on the brow of a hill. And every time I passed by there, Romana's father, who was a canny old rogue, would be peering out of one of the tiny windows like Noah himself, smoking a cheroot. Romana came over from the Bärenwinkel every afternoon at five, and I often walked to meet her at the bridge. She was then twenty-five at most, and everything about her seemed to me to be of exceptional beauty. She was tall, with a broad, open face and water-grey eyes and as much flaxen hair as a Haflinger pony. She differed in every respect from the womenfolk of W., who were almost without exception small, dark, thin-haired and mean. She was so unlike the other women and maids that no one, despite her conspicuous beauty, ever made a proposal of marriage to her. If, later in the evening, I was allowed down into the taproom again to fetch a packet of Zuban cigarettes for my father, Romana would be sailing through the throng of peasants and woodcutters, who would regularly be sozzled by nine, as if she came from another world. At night the taprooms made a fearsome impression, and if it had not been for Romana I would probably not have dared enter that dreadful place where the menfolk sat hunched on the long benches with a vacant look in their eyes. Occasionally one of these motionless figures would rise and sway, as if he were on a raft, towards the door that opened onto the hallway. There were pools of beer and melted snow on the oiled floorboards, and the smoke, drifting through the bar in dense swathes towards the rattling ventilator, joined with the sour reek of wet leather and loden cloaks and spilled gentian schnapps. Mounted on the walls above the brown-painted panelling, stuffed martens, lynxes, capercaillies, vultures and other exterminated creatures were awaiting the time until they could take their long overdue revenge. The peasants and woodcutters almost always sat together in groups at the top or bottom ends of the bar. In the middle stood the large iron stove, which quite often in the winter months was stoked and poked so much that it started to glow. The only one who sat alone, unheeded by all the others, was Hans Schlag the huntsman of whom it was said that he hailed from other parts, from Koßgarten on the Neckar in fact, and that he had managed extensive hunting grounds in the Black Forest for several years before moving from there to the district around W., nobody knew precisely why. He had been out of work for over a year until he had been taken on by the Bavarian forestry commission. Schlag the hunter was a fine figure of a man, with dark, curly hair and beard and uncommonly deep-set, brooding eyes. For hours, frequently until far into the night, he would sit with his half-emptied tankard without exchanging a word with anyone. His dog, Waldmann, slept at his feet, tied to the rucksack hanging from the back of the chair. Whenever I went down into the taproom to fetch a packet of Zuban for my father, Schlag the hunter would be sitting at his table like that. His eyes were always lowered, looking at the gold pocket-watch, an exceptionally fine piece, which he had placed in front of him, as if there were some important appointment he had to keep; but in between times he would look across through his half-closed eyes at Romana, who would be standing behind the high bar filling the schnapps and beer glasses. On one evening that has remained startlingly clear in my memory, at the beginning of December, when snow had fallen as far down as the valley for the first time, the hunter was not sitting in his place when I came into the taproom after supper, and Romana, inexplicably, was nowhere to be seen either. Intending to fetch the packet of five Zuban from the Adlerwirt, I went through the rear of the house out into the yard. A myriad minute crystals glittered in the snow all around me and in the sky above glittered the stars. The headless giant Orion with his short shimmering sword was just rising from behind the black-blue shadow of the mountains. I remained standing for a long time amid that winter splendour, listening to the ringing of the cold and the sound the heavenly lights made in their slow orbits. I suddenly had a feeling then that something was moving in the open doorway of the woodshed. It was Schlag the hunter, who, holding onto the slatted frame of the shed with one hand, stood there in the darkness like a man leaning into the wind, his entire body moving to a strange, consistent and undulating rhythm. Between him and the slatting he gripped with his left hand, Romana lay on a heap of cut turf, and her eyes, as I could make out in the light reflected from the snow, were turned sideways and as wide open as those of Dr Rambousek when his head had lain lifeless on the top of his desk.

From deep in the hunter's chest came a heavy moaning and panting, his frosty breath rose from his beard, and time after time, when the wave surged through the small of his back, he thrust into Romana, while she, for her part, clung closer and closer to him, until the hunter and Romana were but one single indivisible form. I do not think that Romana or Schlag had any idea that I was there. Only Waldmann saw me. Fastened as always to his master's rucksack, he stood quietly behind him on the ground and looked across at me. That same night, around one or two o'clock, the one-legged Engelwirt landlord Sallaba destroyed the entire furnishings and fittings of the bar. When I went to school the following morning, the whole floor was ankle-deep in broken glass. It was a scene of utter devastation. Even the new revolving display cabinet for the Waldbaur chocolates, which reminded me of the tabernacle in church because it could be rotated, had been ripped from the bar and hurled right across the room. Things were not much better outside in the passage. Frau Sallaba was sitting on the cellar steps, crying her eyes out. All the doors were wide open, even the enormous door, fit for a bank vault, that led into the ice store, inside which the ice, stacked in big blocks one on top of the other for the summer, glinted a pale shade of blue. At the sight of the open ice store, or rather at the memory of this sight, it suddenly came to me that, whenever I stepped into the ice store with Romana, I imagined us being locked in there by accident and that, holding each other tight, we would freeze to death, life ebbing out of our bodies as slowly and silently as ice melts in the warmth of the sun.

At school Fräulein Rauch, who meant no less to me than Romana, wrote up on the blackboard in her even hand-writing the chronicle of the calamities which had befallen W. over the ages and underneath it drew a burning house in coloured chalk. The children in the class sat bent over their exercise books, looking up every so often to decipher the faint, faraway letters with screwed-up eyes as they copied, line by line, the long list of terrible events which, when recorded in this way, had something reassuring and comforting about them. In 1511 the Black Death claimed 105 lives. In 1530, 100 houses went up in flames. 1569: the whole settlement devastated in a blaze. 1605: another fire reduced 140 houses to ashes. 1633: W. burned down by the Swedes. 1635: 700 inhabitants died of the plague. 1806–14: 19 volunteers from W. fell in the wars of liberation. 1816–17: years of famine in consequence of unprecedented rainfall. 1870–71: 5 fusiliers from W. lost their lives in battle. 1893: on the 16th of April a great conflagration destroyed the entire village. 1914–18: 68 of our sons laid down their lives for the fatherland. 1939–45: 125 from our ranks did not return home from the Second World War. In the quiet of the classroom the nibs of our pens scratched across the paper. Fräulein Rauch walked along the rows in her tight-fitting green skirt. Whenever she came close to me, I could feel my heart pounding in my throat. That day it never grew light outside. The greyness of the early hours lasted almost until noon and was followed immediately by a gradual nightfall. Even now, at one o'clock, half an hour before school ended for the day, the lights had to be on in the classroom. The white luminous globes hanging from the ceiling and the rows of children bent over their work were reflected in the darkened window-panes through whose mirrored surface the just discernible tops of the apple trees were like black coral in the depths of the ocean. All day an unwonted silence had spread out and taken possession of us. Not even when the caretaker at the end of the last lesson rang the bell in the hall did we break into our customary uproar; rather, we got up without a sound and packed our things away in an orderly fashion without so much as a murmur. Fräulein Rauch helped this or that child, struggling in thick winter clothes, to straighten the satchel on his back.

The schoolhouse stood on a rise at the edge of the village, and, as always when we came out at lunchtime, on that, for me, memorable day too, I looked over the open valley to my left across the rooftops to the forested foothills, behind which arose the jagged rocky ridge of the Sorgschrofen. The houses and farmsteads, the fields, the empty roads and tracks – all was deadened and still under a thin dusting of white. Above us hung the leaden sky, as low and heavy as it only ever is before a great fall of snow. If you put your head right back and stared long enough into that incomprehensible void, you could believe you saw the first flurries of snow swirling out of it. My way took me past the teacher's house and the curate's house and by the high cemetery wall, at the end of which St George was forever driving a spear through the throat of the griffin-like winged creature lying at his feet. From there I had to go down Church Hill and along the so-called Upper Street. A smell of burnt horn

came from the smithy. The forge fire had died down, and the tools, the heavy hammers, tongs and rasps were lying abandoned all round. In W., noon was the hour of things deserted. The water in the tub, into which the blacksmith, when working at his anvil would plunge the red-hot iron so that it hissed, was so calm, and shone so darkly in the pale light that fell on its surface from the open gateway, it was as though no one had ever disturbed it, as though it were destined to remain preserved in this inviolate state for ever. In the shop where Köpf the barber practised his trade, the padded chair with its extendable headrest stood abandoned. The cut-throat razor lay open on the marbled top of the washstand. Since father had returned home from the war, I was sent once a month to have my hair cut, and nothing frightened me more than old Köpf setting about shaving the fuzz from my neck with that freshly stropped knife. The fear became so deeply engrained in me that many years later, when I first saw a representation of the scene in which Salome bears in the severed head of John the Baptist on a silver platter, my thoughts immediately turned to Köpf. To this day I cannot bring myself to enter a barber's, and that I should have gone of my own accord a few years ago at Santa Lucia station in Venice to have my overnight stubble removed still strikes me as a bizarre aberration. The fear that seized me at the sight of Köpf's cabinet gave way to feelings of hope when I paused in front of the small co-op to gaze into the display window at the golden pyramid constructed by Frau Unsinn, the shopkeeper, entirely of Sanella margarine cubes, a sort of pre-Christmas miracle which, every day on my way home from school, touched me like a beacon heralding the new age which was now about to begin even in W. In contrast to the golden sheen on the Sanella cubes, everything else you could buy in Frau Unsinn's shop, the flour in the barrel, the soused herrings in the large tin drum, the pickled gherkins, the massive block of ersatz honey which resembled an iceberg, the blue patterned packets of chicory coffee, and the Emmental cheese wrapped in a damp cloth, seemed to have passed into oblivion. The Sanella pyramid, I knew, towered into the future, and while, before my mind's eye, it grew higher and higher, so high that it almost reached up to the heavens, a vehicle such as I had never seen appeared at the far end of the deserted Long Road which I had now reached. It was a lilac limousine with a lime-green roof and huge tail fins. Infinitely slow and quite soundless it came gliding towards me. Inside, at the ivory-coloured steering wheel, sat a black man who showed me his teeth, also ivory-coloured, grinning as he went past, perhaps because I was the only living soul he had seen while driving through this remote place. Since among the little clay figures assembled round our Christmas manger, it was the black-faced one of the three Magi who wore a purple cloak with a lime-green border, there was no doubt in my mind that the driver of the car that had drifted past me at that sombre midday hour was none other than King Melchior, and that he bore with him in the vast boot of his streamlined lilac limousine several ounces of gold, a frankincense caddy and an ebony box filled with myrrh. It may well be that I became quite convinced of this only later when, in the afternoon, I re-imagined that scene in the minutest detail as the snow began to fall more and more heavily and I sat at the window watching it twirl down without cease from on high and covering everything by nightfall, the stacks of firewood, the chopping block, the roof of the shed, the redcurrant bushes, the water trough and the kitchen garden in the nunnery next door.

On the following morning, the light still burning in the kitchen, my grandfather came in from clearing paths and told us that word had just reached him from Jungholz that Schlag the hunter had been found dead a good hour's walk beyond his hunting ground, on the Tyrolean side of the border, at the bottom of a ravine. He had evidently fallen while crossing by the narrow footbridge which was dangerous even in summer, and as good as impassable in winter, said my grandfather, waiting as he did every day till my mother was not watching to pour down the sink the milky coffee which was always kept for him on the hotplate of the range. In my grandfather's opinion it was out of the question that Schlag, who must have known his own territory like the back of his hand, should have ended up on the other side purely by mistake. By the same token, nobody knew what the hunter, if he had deliberately gone out of his way, had been doing there, over the Austrian border, at this time of year of all times and with the weather closing in. Whichever way you looked at it, concluded my grandfather, it was a queer and perplexing business. I, for my part, was not able to get the matter out of my mind all day long. When I was at my schoolwork, all I had to do was lower my eyelids a little and I beheld Schlag the hunter lying dead at the bottom of the ravine. And so it was no surprise to me when, at midday, I came upon him on my way home from school. I had heard the jingling of a horse's harness for some time before, out of the grey air and the gently swirling snow, a woodcutters' sledge drawn by the heavy bay belonging to the proprietor of the sawmill, appeared, bearing upon it what was plainly the body of a man under a wine-coloured horse blanket. The sledge, led by the saw-mill proprietor and accompanied by the Jungholz gendarme, halted at the crossroads at the very moment when Dr Piazolo approached, as if by pre-arrangement, ploughing through the knee-deep snow astride his Zündapp. Dr Piazolo, who had evidently already been informed of the tragedy that had occurred, switched the engine off and walked over to the sledge. He drew the blanket down halfway, and beneath it, in what one might say was a peculiarly relaxed posture, there indeed lay the body of the hunter Hans Schlag from Koßgarten on the Neckar. His grey-green attire was hardly disturbed, quite as though nothing had happened. One might have supposed that Schlag had simply fallen asleep, had it not been for the dreadful pallor of his face and the wild hair and beard, streaked with frost and hard as ice. Dr Piazolo had taken off his black motorcycle gloves and, with a cautiousness uncharacteristic in him, was feeling different parts of the body, gone rigid with the cold and rigor mortis, which had set in some time ago. He voiced a suspicion that the hunter, who did not seem to have been injured, had to all appearances initially survived the fall from the footbridge. It was quite possible, he said, that the hunter had lost consciousness through sheer fright at the moment when he slipped, and that his fall had been broken by the saplings growing in the ravine. Death probably did not occur until some time afterwards, as a result of exposure. The gendarme, who had followed Dr Piazolo's conjectures and concurred with them, now reported for his part that the unfortunate Waldmann, who now lay as stiff as a poker at the feet of the hunter, had in point of fact still been alive when the tragedy was discovered. In his opinion, the gendarme said, the hunter had put the dachshund in his rucksack before crossing the bridge, and the rucksack had somehow been dislodged during the fall, for it was found a short distance away, with a trail leading from it across to Schlag, by whose side the dachshund had dug through the snow into the forest floor, which was frozen only on the surface. Strangely enough, as soon as the hunter and his dog had been approached, Waldmann had suddenly gone raving mad, even though there was little more than a breath of life left in him, and he had to be shot there and then. Dr Piazolo bent down once more over the hunter, fascinated, it seemed, by the fact that the snowflakes lay on his face without melting. Then he carefully pulled the horse blanket up over the motionless figure, whereupon, triggered by God knows what slight touch or movement, the repeating watch in the hunter's waistcoat pocket played a bar or so of the song

"Üb immer Treu und Redlichkeit". The men looked at each other with expressions of bewilderment. Dr Piazolo shook his head and climbed onto his motorcycle. The sledge moved on and, still unobserved, I slowly walked the rest of my way home. I have since learned that an autopsy was carried out on the body of Schlag the hunter, who apparently had no relatives of any sort, at the district hospital; it did not, however, yield any further insight beyond the cause of death already established by Dr Piazolo, except for the fact, described in the post-mortem report as curious, that a sailing ship was tattooed on the left upper arm of the dead man.

Shortly before Christmas, a few days after the encounter with the dead hunter, I succumbed to a grave illness which Dr Piazolo and a physician from the nearest town, whom he consulted, diagnosed as diphtheria. Confined to my bed, I lay there, my throat becoming increasingly sore until at length it felt raw and torn open inside and I was fearfully convulsed every few minutes by a cough that racked my chest and my whole body. My limbs, once the illness had me in its grip, seemed so heavy to me that I could no longer raise either my head or my legs or arms, indeed not even my hands. Deep within my body I felt an immense pressure, as if my organs were being put through a mangle.

Again and again I saw before me the village blacksmith
with his tongs pulling my heart, licked by blue flames like
St Elmo's fire, out of the glowing embers and plunging it
into a bucket of ice-cold water. The headache alone forced
me sometimes to the limits of consciousness, but it was not
until the illness reached its climax, when my temperature
had risen to a fraction below the critical point, that delirium
saved me from the worst extremes of pain. As though in
the middle of a desert I lay in a shimmer of heat, my lips
cracked and grey and flaking and in my mouth the foul
taste of the rotting skin in my throat. My grandfather
dripped luke-warm water into my mouth, and I felt it
slowly trickling down across the scorched patches inside
my throat. Time and again, in my delirium, I saw myself
gingerly stepping past Frau Sallaba, who sat weeping on
the stairs that led down into the cellar, and there, in
the furthermost, darkest corner, opening the door of the
cupboard where preserved eggs were kept for winter months
in a large earthenware crock. I put my hand and forearm
through the chalky surface of the water almost to the
bottom of the container, and to my horror I felt that what
was stored in this pot was not eggs safely sequestered, each
one of them, in its shell, but something soft, something
that slipped through my fingers and which I instantly

knew could only be eyeballs gouged from their sockets. Dr Piazolo, who at the onset of my illness had ordered my room to be turned into a quarantine ward which only my grandfather and mother were allowed to enter, had me swathed from head to toe in dampened warm sheets, which at first proved beneficial, but, because of the constriction, soon gave rise in me to panic and fear. Twice a day my mother had to wash the floor with vinegar water, and until dusk fell the windows of my sickward were kept wide open so that at times the snow drifted in almost as far as the middle of the room, and my grandfather would sit by my bed in his overcoat with his hat on his head. The illness ran its course over two weeks, until after Christmas, even when Epiphany had come round I could scarcely eat anything other than spoonfuls of bread and milk. The door to the quarantine ward was now left ajar, and some of those who lived and worked in our house took turns to put in an appearance at the threshold, including Romana a couple of times, gaping at this boy who, by dint of a miracle, had just escaped with his life. It was already Lent before I was allowed to go into the garden occasionally. For the time being, a return to school was ruled out. In the spring, for two hours a day, I was placed in the care of my teacher, Fräulein Rauch. Fräulein Rauch was the daughter of the chief forester, so every afternoon I went across to the shingled villa which stood in a small arboretum and was both the forestry commission's district office and the chief forester's home. There, when the weather was cold, I would sit with my teacher on the bench by the stove and on sunny days outside in the revolving summer-house under the trees, completely devoted to the tasks I was set, filling my exercise books with a web of lines and numbers in which I hoped to entangle Fräulein Rauch for ever.

I had spent the better part of a month, till the beginning of December, in W., and for more or less the entire time I had been the only guest at the Engelwirt inn. Only occasionally did one of those solitary commercial travellers appear, who spend the evenings in the bar room finishing off their day's work, calculating percentages and rates of commission. As I too was forever bent over my papers, they may well, at first, have taken me for another salesman but, after a closer look at my outward appearance, they probably decided that mine was a different and perhaps more dubious profession. Disturbed not so much by this scrutiny as by the first preparations that were being made in the house for the beginning of the winter season, I resolved to leave, particularly as my writing had reached the point at which I either had to continue for ever or break off. The following day, after changing several times and spending lengthy periods waiting on the platforms of draughty provincial stations – I cannot remember anything about this journey other than the grotesque figure of a middleaged chap of gigantic proportions who was wearing a hideous, modishly styled Trachten suit and a broad tie with multi-coloured bird feathers sewn onto it, which were ruffled by the wind – on that day, with W. already far behind me, I sat in the Hook of Holland express travelling through the German countryside, which has always been alien to me, straightened out and tidied up as it is to the last square inch and corner. Everything appeared to be appeased and numbed in some sinister way, and this sense of numbness soon came over me also. I did not care to open the newspapers that I had bought, or to drink the mineral water that was there before me. Stretches of grassland swept past on either side and ploughed fields in which the pale green winter wheat had emerged according to schedule; neatly delineated fir-tree plantations, gravel pits, football pitches, industrial estates, and the ever-expanding colonies of family homes behind their rustic fences and privet hedges, all of them painted in that slightly greyish shade of white which has become the preferred colour of the nation. As I looked out, it made me uneasy that not a soul was to be seen anywhere, though enough vehicles were speeding along the wet roads veiled in dense mists of spray. Even in the streets of the towns, there were far more cars than people. It was as if mankind had already made way for another species, or had fallen under a kind of curfew. The silence of my fellow passengers sitting motionless in the air-conditioned express carriage did nothing to dispel such conjectures, but as I looked out at the passing landscape which had been so thoroughly parcelled up and segmented, the words "south-west Germany", "south-west Germany" were running over and over in my mind, till after a couple of hours of mounting irritation I came to the conclusion that something like an eclipse of my mental faculties was about to occur.

The compulsive fixation did not wear off until the train pulled into Heidelberg station, where there were so many people crowding the platforms that I feared they were fleeing from a city doomed or already laid waste. The last to come into my compartment of those passengers who had just boarded was a young woman wearing a beret of brown velvet whom I instantly recognised, without a shadow of a doubt, as Elizabeth, daughter of James I, who according to the chronicles travelled to Heidelberg as the bride of the Elector Palatine and, during the short period in which she held court there in great splendour, became known as the Winter Queen. No sooner had she sat down and settled herself into her corner than this young woman was deeply immersed in a book entitled *The Seas of Bohemia*, written by an authoress unknown to me by the name of Mila Stern. Only when we were travelling alongside the Rhine did she occasionally look up from her reading and glance out through the window at the river and the steep slopes of the opposite bank. A stiff northerly wind must have sprung up, because the flags on the barges that were ploughing their way upstream through the grey waters were not flying backwards from the stern but forwards, as in a child's drawing, and this lent the scene something that was at once touching and awry. The light outside had steadily diminished, and the great river valley was now filled with a faint luminescence. I stepped out into the corridor. The slate- and violet-coloured vineyards, hatched into the hillsides, were covered here and there with turquoise bird-netting. Snow now began to drift by, scoring delicate slanting lines over a view which was constantly changing as we slid past yet always remained the same. Suddenly I felt we were on our way to the far north, approaching the furthermost tip of the island of Hokkaido. The Winter Queen, who I believed had brought about this

transformation of the Rhine landscape, had also come out
into the corridor, and had already been standing watching
the beautiful scene for some time at my side before I
heard her reciting, entirely to herself, as it seemed to me,
the following lines, with a long-lost inflexion in her voice:

> Grasses white as driven snow
> Veils far blacker than a crow
> Gloves as tender as the rose
> Masks for faces no one knows.

That I did not know what to respond at the time, did not
know how this winter verse continued, and, despite the
feelings within me, could not say a word but merely
stood there stupid and mute, looking out onto a world that
was now almost gone in the fading twilight, is something
which, since that day, I have often much regretted. Presently
the Rhine valley opened out, gleaming apartment blocks
appeared on the plain, and the train drew into Bonn, where
the Winter Queen, without my having been able to say even
a word to her, got out. Time and again since then, I have
attempted to find that book, *The Seas of Bohemia*; but
though it is undoubtedly of the greatest importance for me,
it is, alas, not listed in any bibliography, in any catalogue,
or indeed anywhere at all.

The following afternoon, back in London, my first port of call was the National Gallery. The painting by Pisanello that I wanted to see was not in its usual place, but owing to renovation work had been hung in a poorly lit room in the basement into which few of the visitors who wandered the gallery every day found their way. It is a small painting, measuring about 30 by 50 centimetres, lamentably imprisoned in a far too heavy Victorian frame. The upper half of the picture is almost completely filled by a golden disc, radiant against the blue of the sky and serving as a background for the Virgin and her Redeemer Child. Lower down runs a line of dark green treetops from one side to the other. On the left stands the patron saint of herds, herdsmen and lepers, St Anthony. He is wearing a dark red cowled habit and a capacious earthen-brown cloak. In his hand he holds a bell. Beside him lies a tame boar, close against the ground in kindly submission. The hermit with a stern expression surveys the shining knight who stands before him, and who, for his part, is all of this world, almost heart-rendingly so. The dragon, a ringed and winged creature, has already breathed its last. The ornate armour, wrought of white metal, draws the evening light unto it. Not the slightest shadow of guilt shows on the youthful face of St George. His neck and throat are bared to us, unprotected. The most remarkable feature, however, is the very finely worked broad-brimmed straw hat adorned with a large feather which the knight wears on his head. I wish I could know how Pisanello conceived the idea of furnishing St George with such inappropriate and positively extravagant headgear. *San Giorgio con cappello di paglia* – most odd indeed, as the two trusty horses gazing across the knight's shoulder may well be thinking too.

I made my way back from the National Gallery to Liverpool Street station on foot. As I did not want to walk along the Strand and then down Fleet Street, I negotiated the labyrinth of smaller streets above these busy thoroughfares; Chandos Place, Maiden Lane and Tavistock Street took me to Lincoln's Inn Fields and from there, via Holborn Circus and the Holborn Viaduct, I reached the western perimeter of the City. I cannot have covered much more than three miles, yet I felt as if I had never walked so far in my life than on that afternoon. I became fully aware of my fatigue, however, only as I paused at the threshold of an underground station, from which came the familiar sweetish, dusty warmth of the subterranean world, and, as I stood there, detected, like a scent which might stir the imaginings of an oarsman far out to sea, the faint perfume of the white, pink and russet-red chrysanthemums being sold at the entrance by a man with something of Prospero about him. I then realised that this was the station where, on my frequent journeys by tube, no one ever embarked or alighted. The train would stop, the doors open; one looked out onto the deserted platform and heard the warning "Mind the gap"; the doors would close again, and the train move off. Whenever I had travelled through that station it had been the same, and on not one occasion did any of the other passengers so much as raise an eyebrow. Evidently it was only I who found this strange circumstance unnerving. So now I stood on the pavement before the entrance to that very station and, if I were not to walk that last tiring stretch, I had only to enter the dark ticket hall where, apart from a black woman sitting in her inspector's box, there was no sign of life. Although I stood there for a considerable time, on the very brink so to speak, and even exchanged a few glances with the black inspector, I did not dare to take the final step.

The train rolled slowly out of Liverpool Street station, past the soot-stained brick walls the recesses of which have always seemed to me like parts of a vast system of catacombs that comes to the surface there. In the course of time a multitude of buddleias, which thrive in the most inauspicious conditions, had taken root in the gaps and cracks of the nineteenth-century brickwork. The last time I went past those black walls, on my way to Italy in the summer, the sparse shrubs were just flowering. And I could hardly believe my eyes, as the train was waiting at a signal, to see a yellow brimstone butterfly flitting about from one purple flower to the other, first at the top, then at the bottom, now on the left, constantly moving. But that was many months ago, and this butterfly memory was perhaps prompted only by a wishful thought. There was no room for doubt, however, about the reality of my poor fellow travellers, who had all set off early that morning neatly turned out and spruced up, but were now slumped in their seats like a defeated army and, before they turned to their newspapers, were staring out at the desolate forecourts of the metropolis with fixed unseeing eyes. Soon, where the wilderness of buildings thinned out a little, three tall blocks of flats entirely boxed in scaffolding and surrounded by uneven patches of grass became visible at some distance, while much further off, before the blazing strip of sky on the western horizon, rain fell like a great funeral pall from the dark-blue cloud that hung over the entire city. When the train changed track, I was able to glance back at the great towers of the City, rising far above everything around them, the topmost storeys gilded by the rays of the sun slanting in from the west. The suburbs swept past – Arden, Forest Gate, Maryland – before we reached the open countryside. The light over the western horizon was gradually extinguished. The shadows of evening were already settling on the fields and hedgerows. Idly I turned the pages of an India paper edition of Samuel Pepys's diary, Everyman's Library, 1913, which I had purchased that afternoon, and read passages at random in this 1,500-page account, until drowsiness overcame me and I found myself going over the same few lines again and again without any notion what they meant. And then I dreamed that I was walking through a mountainous terrain. A white roadway of finely crushed stone stretched far ahead and in endless hairpins went on and up through the woods and finally, at the top of the pass, led through a deep cutting across to the other side of the high range, which I recognised in my dream as the Alps. Everything I saw from up there was of the same chalky colour, a bright, glaring grey in which a myriad of quartz fragments glimmered, as if the rocks, by a force deep inside them, were being dissolved into radiant light. From my vantage-point the road continued downward, and in the distance a second range of mountains at least as lofty as the first one arose, which I feared I would not be able to cross. To my left there was a drop into truly vertiginous depths. I walked to the edge of the road, and knew that I had never gazed down into such chasms before. Not a tree was there to be seen, not a bush, not even a stunted shrub or a tussock of grass: there was nothing but ice-grey shale. The shadows of the clouds scudded across the steep slopes and through the ravines. The silence was absolute, for even the last traces of plant life, the last rustling leaf or strip of bark, were long gone, and only the stones lay unmoved upon on the ground. Into that breathless void, then, words returned to me as an echo that had almost faded away – fragments from the account of the Great Fire of London as recorded by Samuel Pepys. We saw the fire grow. It was not bright, it was a gruesome, evil, bloody flame, sweeping, before the wind, through all the City. Pigeons lay destroyed upon the pavements, in hundreds, their feathers singed and burned. A crowd of looters roams through Lincoln's Inn. The churches, houses, the woodwork and the building stones, ablaze at once. The churchyard yews ignited, each one a lighted torch, a shower of sparks now tumbling to the ground. And Bishop Braybrooke's grave is opened up, his body disinterred. Is this the end of time? A muffled, fearful, thudding sound, moving, like waves, throughout the air. The powder house exploded. We flee onto the water. The glare around us everywhere, and yonder, before the darkened skies, in one great arc the jagged wall of fire. And, the day after, a silent rain of ashes, westward, as far as Windsor Park.